Ark

A novel by John Heldon

ISBN: 1466446226

ISBN-13: 9781466446229

Library of Congress Control Number: 2011918992

CreateSpace, North Charleston, SC

Disclaimer

This book is a work of fiction. The events, characters, locales, establishments, roadways, etc., are products of the author's imagination. They are solely meant for the entertainment of the reader, and any resemblance to reality is purely coincidental.

To Ginni, Geoff, Ev, John, and Laney

Acknowledgments

I need to thank my mother and father, those "octo youths" who have continued to give me encouragement since the day I was born.

To my wife and son, who have put up with my irritability and distance during this process.

Again to my wife, my in-house editor, whose keen eyes never miss what mine did.

To Calvin Barry Schwartz, author of *Vichy Water*, for his encouragement and willingness to offer any and all help he could give me.

To Barry Sheinkopf of the Writing Center in Englewood Cliffs, N.J. Thank you for planting the slow growing seed about twenty years ago, which finally bloomed this day.

To the Taub brothers, Jordan and Benjamin. Jordan, for cover design help, and Jamie, for invaluable advice and counsel regarding publication.

John J. Heldon, Jr. October, 2011

"When a muse amuses you, remember to share the feeling with others."

Me

Prologue

The Men's Basketball Back Court, a booster club for the sport, was winding down its meeting. The question and answer area, where my interest barometer always swings between tedium and insightfulness, was on life support as far as I was concerned. A couple of dumb questions in a row had me starting to doze, then begin fumbling for my car keys and glancing at the exit.

The next question came from a booming voice seated a knight move, or two seats right and one row ahead, of me. The voice belonged to a big, hulking guy, obviously a former player, about my age, which put his dunking days far behind him.

I don't remember the question he asked. I just remember he interjected that his blog was up to one hundred thousand hits. Wow! I thought. I had just started a blog a few months before, finally finding the time in my retirement that I couldn't find in my working life to pursue a writing career. I decided to write anecdotal, funny stories about our family, sort of a written oral history, which present and perhaps future family might find amusing. Without trying to ring the bell "hit" wise, forwarding new stories as they were published to friends and family, I was up to five hundred hits. I didn't care about my hits. I was having fun, and beginning to feel good about writing for the long term.

Instead of bee-lining toward the exit, I tacked over and introduced myself to Calvin, the one- hundred-thousand-hit man. He turned out to be a very gregarious, engaging person, genuinely interested in what interested me. I quickly switched the subject from basketball to writing as we walked to our cars. Already a book author, he offered to impart what he'd learned over the years plying his craft. A really nice guy. Just met, and he's eager to help me. None of us are good judges of character all the time. I've had good gut feelings before about someone, and have been wrong, but I was pretty sure about Calvin.

As we approached our cars, we established some background. Where did you grow up? Where do you live now?

"No shit!!" we both said together. Same town. Walking distance. This makes it convenient to car pool to the Summer League basketball games at the Delaware shore, a half hour away, and to continue to talk about our writing.

The day the Summer League schedule was published, Calvin beat me to it. I saw his email as I logged on to send him one. I responded, agreeing we should go to the season opener. We would meet at his house. He offered to drive, and we would happily zoom toward the shore venue. Happily I say, because that day, July 6th, was the beginning of the basketball season for us fanatics.

Cal was very emphatic about how his writing, and the idea for his first book, came to him.

"Like a thunderbolt," he said. "It all came to me at once. The idea of writing, and the whole book flashed into my mind at once."

I found this very spiritual, and understood that it happens often to great artists who create works that, for the rest of time, earn them the genius moniker. Handel, the composer, wrote *Messiah* in twenty-four days. Frank Lloyd Wright, the architect, shook the plans for *Fallingwater*, that many consider to be the most famous house in America, out of his sleeve in two-and-a-half hours, while his clients were in route to see them.

I wasn't counting on that happening to me; or that Cal or I would ever become literary geniuses. After that first meeting with Cal, there was a ferocious thunderstorm that night. One bolt went from my eye to my ear in a split second. Close, I thought, but not close enough to give me my “novel” idea. I’m going to have to give birth to the book. Slow growing. Expanding. Lots of kicking and screaming. In labor for a long time, but in the end,

“It’s a book!”

The idea wasn’t a thunderbolt, but a lens coming into focus. That chance meeting with Cal opened a vista of words clearly flowing to my consciousness. That’s how this story emerged, and took hold of me.

Chapter One

I needed Sleep. Capital S is for sound, uninterrupted; wake up with energy, Sleep. The story I had in my head, and how I was going to tell it, was pushing me to stay awake for long hours, until I could organize my thoughts, and start tickling the keyboard. Once my mind saw the story more clearly, I started to calm down. Thomas Edison, the inventor, said that ideas are in the air. If so, I had been waiting and waiting for that fresh air that wafted my story toward me. My story…to me and no one else.

The pillow I eased my head down onto felt like a mixture of cloud and downy feathers. As my head settled as far as it would go, I glanced at Genna, my wife (sound asleep), then at the clock, 1:40A.M.

I closed my eyes and started thinking about the Ark. That was the nick name for the old, multi event center at the college I attended forty five years ago. Concerts, assemblies, lectures, and sporting events were all accommodated in *the Ark.* No animals, just people, were herded in for this or that function.

As far as I can tell, the nickname had no religious connotation, and it was derived for purely secular reasons, a place of refuge or asylum. Quite often in college life, refuge and asylum don't mean the same thing. An asylum is where crazy people do crazy things, or crazy things can just happen; at a sporting event, for example.

I think I slept pretty well. I wasn't tired anymore, but I just felt a little, "off," is the best way I can put it. Usually if I wake up and haven't slept well, it takes a while for my head to clear, before getting up to speed. If I sleep well, my brain zooms back onto life's highway quickly. This wakeup was somewhere in between. I was rested, but curiously still thinking about the Ark, the same thought I'd had when I started to recharge.

My first encounter with the Ark was at Freshman Assembly Orientation, where we all got the "you or one of your seatmates on either side won't be here next semester" speech. A very cute reality check welcome, if not a confidence booster.

If you mention the Ark to any alum of my generation, however, a sporting event will come to their mind first, most likely, Men's Basketball. That's because Men's Basketball started to gain fanatic interest while I was at the school, and nearly achieved championship status a few years later. By light of day, the Ark is still a magnificent, imposing structure, a Federalist style leviathan with a brick facade, and rows of windows with thick molded scrolls above each. All of the ornate molding around the windows is still painted white, as is the soaring cupola with its bronzed weather vane centered in the middle. To dispel its uniqueness, it was probably one of thousands of such buildings on college campuses across the country. However, I decided to forego these architectural details, and to visit the Ark (I only live a half hour away) late one night as I was driving home. I decided to go late, hoping that no one was there. It would be quiet, and I just might find an unlocked door to gain entrance. Sure enough, a lazy janitor or a careless student left a back door for me to return and reminisce in the old Ark's darkened quietude.

There were enough night lights for me to drift into the building without needing cat eyes to see. The only sound was my light clicking heels on the wooden floor. I was trying to tiptoe in case someone authorized to be there wouldn't hear me. Looking down, I saw the faint outline of the center court circle where basketball history had been made. This was the perfect spot to pan the innards of the old place, and I could just barely make out the white painted railings and sky blue seats in the balcony, the familiar school colors. In the darkness, I was beginning to feel like Jonah in the belly of that old whale. I kept glancing around, trying to remember the places I used to sit when I first became a basketball junkie. As I picked out a few seats, I must have imagined hearing a slight squeak, the sound of a sneaker on a high gloss court. Nah, this antique of a building must have a variety of sounds all its own, from years of standing up to wind, rain, snow, as well as the heel pounding from legions of students for ninety years. After I rationalized that, I heard a few more of those squeaks getting slightly louder, as if coming towards me. Creepy, I thought. The old Ark is playing with me. Then, all of a sudden, really creepy. A gust of air (I'm still inside, right?), goose bumps down my back, from my head to my heels, and, what felt like a tap on the shoulder. Shit, I thought, a creepy night watchman is onto me. I slowly turned around, trying to conjure an innocent explanation. My first word stuck to my palate as I saw, not a man, but a glowing figure, more like an apparition.

I started to shake like I'd been tasered, barely able to stand. My mind raced, trying to assess what was happening. I thought in rapid succession:

"What did I do now, God?"

"I'm not like the little boy at Fatima!"

"What did I eat for supper to cause this?"

Now sweating, and still struggling to remain upright, I was given a sense of calm from one word spoken by this ghost before me.

"Hi."

He just stood there quietly as he watched my chest sucking and heaving volumes of air my lungs never handled before. As I switched from panic to "there's an explanation" mode, I suddenly realized that I knew this guy, but he probably didn't know me.

"Slick? I said.

"That's me, and how does your sorry old ass know who I am? How can you see and hear me? I was just going to play with you. I didn't expect you to answer back."

Realizing I startled him as much as he did me helped my spasms to relax their grip even further. Even though I didn't have half a clue what was going on, I was now relaxed, and had to chuckle. The ghost right in front of me was Slick Sampson, just as he appeared in his playing days forty years ago, on this very court, right down to the short shorts that were fashionable in those days. The rest of his uniform was vintage 1971, including the high socks and high-top sneakers. He still had the same moustache and medium afro. He had that kind of kinky hair, even though he was White. He was maybe six feet tall in sneakers, but he played taller, able to grab the rim with both hands. Slick was not short for a given name, but for his style of play on the court. He was lightening quick, slipping effortlessly through screens and picks on defense, and had a jump shot that only knew the inside of the net. Opposing players were afraid of him most when he got behind them, fearing a ball poke from their blind side. He was silicone in motion, known for his brashness and arrogance, which he backed up, of course. He was funny back then, and the way he queried me now made me laugh like old times.

"I said, how do you know who I am, and why are you laughing at me?"

"Slick," I said, "I went to school here. Everybody who went here that knows basketball, knows you, especially the way you're standing before me, as you were in 1971. I'll go you one better. I know how your sorry old ass, as you put it to me, looks today. In fact, I just saw you a few weeks ago, in 2011. You're bald as a baby's ass, but you can still shoot the ball."

"I know. I know all that. My first step's in the crapper, though. Otherwise, I could still be playin." Slick said, always the comedian.

"Slick," I said. "You got to help me out here. What the hell is going on?"

"I really don't know. Me and my teammates play here all the time. People have been walking around here through the years, right up to the present day, and we don't care. We just play right through'em. We all still love to play, but why over and over? It's like we were sent here for a reason. What really gave me the heeby jeebs a few years ago was we were playing a game while a 2008 summer league game was being played at the same time. That didn't bother me. It was when I looked up in the stands and I see me in 2008 watching the game. It was me watching me! I know I couldn't see me, but it still made me miss my next couple of shots."

I said, incredulously, "Okay, Slick, back up. You said there are more of you. Your teammates. From 1971. How is this possible?"

"It seems not much gets wasted in the Universe. Once events pass in time, they're still out there, floating around like radio waves. They're like files everywhere. 1971 is next to 1972. There's still plenty of room for everything that's ever happened. It's a big, big place, you know, and it's expanding." He paused, and his dead pan delivery broke into a smile.

"I'm just playin' with you, man. I really don't know. Ask me something about basketball. All I know is we keep playing here, as in 1971. Like I said, it's still fun, but I want to know why."

At the same time, I had a queer thought his notions were provocative.

Well, let me get back to the here and now (then?), I wondered. "Slick, where are your teammates?"

"They're showering. I just stayed out to can some free throws. I missed two during the game we just played against Megamont University. We won this time."

Sure enough, I faintly heard water droplets toward the old locker room area.

Wait a minute! Megamont. That was the team they lost to in the NCAA finals of the championship that year, 1971. Sunnyside College, our school, versus Megamont University. As the matchup sounds, it was David vs. Goliath, a real Cinderella story had we pulled it off.

"Slick, you're not saying you can change history?"

"Not really. These games are like scrimmages. We never actually played them again, and what we're doing here doesn't change that. They beat us last week, however."

Slick stepped up to the foul line, dribbled and squatted to prepare his shot.

"Who's there?" boomed and echoed through the Ark.

Slick evaporated in an instant, and I hastily tiptoed toward the corner shadows behind a bleacher. Luckily, the bleacher was folded in, not out, or, "sit ready" for game time. I was able to wedge behind the corner, and peer out through a slot between a seat and a foot rail. The night watchman just had a small pen light to scan the perimeter, and not a ten battery maglite which surely would have caught my reflecting eyes staring back at him.

I then heard bellowing laughter at the foul line where Slick was netting them one after carbon copied other. The night watchman had just walked through him without feeling him or hearing his loud laughter. I grabbed a piece of the bleacher, and squeezed it hard. It felt like wood. It felt real, but it didn't stop me from thinking I was really losing it.

The watchman retreated, shaking his head, now believing HE was hearing things.

I stayed behind the bleachers, and whispered to Slick, "Why did you disappear for a few seconds when the guard came in?"

"I didn't. You just thought I did."

"Great! Now I'm imagining what I'm imagining. Slick, you gotta help me out here."

"Just relax, scarecrow. You must be here, and able to see what you see, for a reason. You're in some kind of zone."

While he's talking to me, he's draining ten foul shots in a row, the last one making the same sound as the others, the friction sound of leather on cord, which is almost indescribable.

"Let's go see if the other guys are ready. You want to meet'em?"

I thought to myself, this is really great. Not only am I seeing a ghost, I'm going to meet more of them. Most ghost stories I've heard about, a ghost just scares the bejesus out of you, then goes away. I'm going to be Ebenezer Scrooge, without the money, and get to follow them. I also noticed that I no longer heard any shower water.

This is nuts, but Slick did say I must be here for a reason.

Great, now I'm letting a ghost lead the way, instead of me running, away. I guess if I wasn't a basketball junkie, I wouldn't be doing this, but I am.

"Sure, Slick, why not?"

"C'mon, tippy toe your old ass over here. Follow me."

He leads me across the court to a side door which leads to the locker room. He opens the door and a burst of light splashes out of it. I hasten to go inside behind Slick, so the door closes again and doesn't attract the attention of the watchman. Once inside, I notice there are no lights on, it's just the glow of many more spirits. The place was lit up like a TV studio.

"Ok, pop quiz," Slick said. "You knew me, scarecrow. Can you name the other starters?"

"Slick, guys, please call me John. I am not nearly as scared as when you tapped me on the shoulder," (and thinking I'm going to ace this test.)

They were all staring at me with the "how'd he get here" look. Each one looked as spooked as I did. Not like Slick upon first seeing me. I guess it helped that I had my back turned toward him, when he approached me. Now, in the locker room, it was spooky stares right back at one another. At the same time, I knew what to expect from them. They didn't know what to expect from me.

"First up, this is your partner in crime in the backcourt, Quincy Wilson."

"Quick" Quincy Wilson was the point guard that sparked this machine of a team to race and swarm over opponents. "Q" was the most incongruous member of the team, a "blue blood" whose lineage went back almost to the Pilgrims on both sides of the family. "Quincy" honored the Adams family on his mother's side, while his father's side boasted a President also. Slick was probably a tad faster, but Q's "wingspan" and height, 6' 7", made up for the split second in question. What he did in tandem with Slick was just short of criminal, generating steal after steal, game after game. "Quick and Slick" each had a knack for getting the opposing ball handler to turn his back; the other one would come from his blind side, swipe the ball, and cruise for a layup, with time for a snack before the defender could recover. Everyone in the gym, except the guy with the ball, knew what was about to happen. Quincy could shoot the ball almost as well as Slick, but he didn't have to. Quincy just had a knack for getting the ball to the player with the easiest shot. His height enabled Q to see the court better, as most matchup players with him were considerably shorter.

"That's Harry Hoppe, "small" forward."

Harry was born with the right last name (the "e" being silent). His blond hair, icy blue eyes, and chiseled features spelled "movie star" when he walked the campus in street clothes. "Small forward" always made me laugh when describing him. It wasn't that he was tall for the position, maybe 6' 4" in sneakers, he just played much taller, and from his nickname, "Hops," you could tell he had mini pogo sticks in the heels of his sneakers. If he wasn't a state high jump champion in track and field, he could have been. There were times I thought he might hit his head on the rim. No shit.

"Next to him is Charlie Bennett."

C.B. was, to make no mistake, the drive shaft of the engine. He had the maturity of a man amongst a bunch of little kids. Charlie wasn't that tall for his position, (6' 4" like Harry), power forward. However, he had broad shoulders and muscles you could see ripple through his suit. His looks you wouldn't call handsome. His sandy brown hair, freckles, and flat crooked nose along with his physique said "get out of my way" to the other team. For him, it was "will" more than "power" which enabled him to do what he did. Any time the team needed a basket, everyone, including the other team, knew C.B. was getting the ball, and he always canned the shot anyway. He never failed the team at crunch time during the regular season.

"This tall, skinny kid is John Bird, the center."

John was the only freshman starter on the team, and the only Black man. Although he developed quite an offensive skill set in future years, all he needed to do was defend on this year's team, much like Bill Russell with those great Boston Celtics. Coincidentally, Johnny grew up in the San Francisco Bay area, probably seeing Russ play his college ball as a kid.

"I'll go you one better, Slick. That other guy is Byron Barrett, the sixth man."

"B.B." was instant offense off the bench. Not an easy task. Most players need a few minutes to get into the flow, and warm up before they can be effective. Not B.B., he would catch and shoot from his spot in the corner. Bombs away, B.B. Nothing but net. As the other freshman on the team, "B.B. gun" played like a junior.

"Ok, Joohhn, as you want us to call you, you passed. No medals given out here, but you can keep hangin' with us, if you want."

"Slick," Charlie said, "how the hell did he get here? You never brought around an old stray dog before."

The others chuckled timidly. They too wanted some answers. Knowing who they were helped me a little, but they not knowing me didn't help them. The other strange thing I noticed was these guys, who had just showered, weren't in street clothes. Instead, they had fresh, clean uniforms on. All but Slick stared at me with laser eyes.

I was NOT feeling the love.

"Slick, maybe I should leave, and come back another time. These other guys seem uneasy in my presence, and I don't want to spook anyone around here." A couple of chuckles from Sampson and a joint smirk from the others made me realize what I just said.

"Why don't I just step away, and come back with a few questions after I've had a chance to digest this on my own. Meanwhile, you can discuss things with your teammates. I can still come back, and be able to see you guys again, right?" It was clear to me that Slick was much more okay with what was happening than the rest of them. He needed time, I thought, to bring them up to speed. Anyway, I really didn't want to be on the wrong side of any of these ghosts.

"I don't see why not, John, you did it once. The first time is usually the hardest, right? C'mon, I'll walk you to the door."

I was hoping he WAS right. What if this was some kind of portal that only opens once, a time and a place, then is gone forever, like so many missed opportunities we've all had. Then I decided to just let this all play out, remembering my wife Genna's credo.

"What will be, will be," she is fond of saying. I'm just hoping it applies to this spirit world I'm now mixed up in.

I tiptoed behind Slick, sure to keep my heels off the court, not wanting a return visit from the watchman.

"Don't worry about that old fool," as if reading my mind, Slick said. (He really couldn't, I hoped). "He's probably back to sleep already."

We approached the same door I had gained entrance through earlier.

"Always come around to this door when you return. I'll leave it open for you again."

I started to whisper goodbye when what he said hit me.

"Wait a second. You left that door open for me tonight?"

"Not just for you, for somebody that could walk through that door, from your here and now, and see and talk to us. I've been hoping for this for a long time, forty years, to be exact. That somebody just happened to be you. I guess that makes you, the ONE. The other guys don't know what I been hoping for and thinking about. I guess now, I have to tell'em."

I was trembling again from this information, however, not taser-like upon first making Slick's acquaintance earlier.

I settled down when I heard Slick say, "John, thank you for coming."

The look in his sleepy, half sad eyes was sincere.

"I'll see you real soon, Slick."

"Please," was all he said.

Chapter Two

The walk to my VW Eos was brisk and emphatically more heel than toe. I chirped the door lock, but before getting in, I glanced toward the window pane of the door I had just left. Was that a faint image of Slick? I couldn't be sure. Just like when I THOUGHT he disappeared before the night watchman showed up.

I don't take any type of sleeping pill, but I've heard some people get behind the wheel, and go for a drive, under their influence. That's how I felt. Some kind of twilight this is, I thought.

Anyway, I slid into that comfy bucket seat of the car that made me feel like a teenager again, buckled up, and zipped out of the lot without looking back again. I weaved through the back streets, entered the ramp to Highway 20 South, and then punched the throttle for a few seconds like I was in a rocket trying to escape gravity. Not seeing cars or cops, I punched it again, hit 95mph, and then coasted back to sanity at 60. I needed that burst, hoping to readjust to reality. It seemed to do the trick. I squeezed the steering wheel, turned on the satellite radio, and glanced at the rest of the dash. Everything inside the car felt real again, not like the inside of the Ark.

The rest of the ride home felt as real as can be. Almost like the trip to the Ark never happened. Almost. I pulled into the garage, turned off the Eos, sent the garage door down, and sat very still for about a minute. I glanced at myself in the rear view mirror, focused my eyes, and faced the fact.

It DID happen.

I decided one thing right then. Genna, my wife, wasn't going to hear any of this just yet, if ever. This all had to stay just with me. If these beans don't stay in the can, I'll be seeing commitment papers in no time. She's probably asleep already, so I'll have 'til the morning to gather my wits and put on my game face. She's a tough one to get by though. Her intuition seismometer can usually detect my feelings half way around the globe. I'll think of something, and in conjunction with making her a nice breakfast, I'll get by.

As I thought, the house was dark when I opened the door, and I quickly tickled the alarm keypad before it could start to scream at me and awaken Genna. I did NOT want to start playing twenty questions with her tonight. After locking the door, I rekeyed the alarm code, then navigated around the known creaky floor boards, and tiptoed (again, tonight) towards "my" bathroom, far enough away from the double master bath that Genna had claimed to be '"hers". Tonight, I was glad to be married to a woman who thought no bathroom was big enough for her to share.

As I went through my customary hygienic routine, I stared at the mirror and began to mentally rehash what went on tonight, and what needed to happen tomorrow.

Oh, screw it! If I start to replay tonight's events, I'll never get to sleep, and If I start planning what I'm going to say at breakfast to Genna, it'll sound too scripted, and I'll be done for. Never mind twenty, how about playing one hundred questions? Better to take Ringo Starr's advice, and "act naturally." I said goodnight to the mirror by turning the bathroom light out, then started to renavigate the floor boards towards the master bedroom.

I can see by the night light, and hear from the silence, that Genna is sleeping on her left side, away from me. This is good news. If she falls asleep on her right side, she snores like a wood chipper, and seems to dream about a kick boxer. The old saying, "opposites attract" applies here. I need to sleep on my right side, or I do the same thing. To insure domestic tranquility, she sleeps left, I sleep right. That's the deal we have together.

I ease under the covers and settle on another soft landing on the pillow. One more thought crosses my mind. I think of St. Anthony, the patron saint for lost articles.

St. Anthony, help me find sleep tonight.

* * *

I hardly ever need an alarm. The light entering our east facing bedroom is usually enough. It seemed to be a nice, sunny day. I like sunny days, or at least mornings, because my exercise of choice is brisk, forty-five minute walks around the neighborhood. This doesn't work for Genna. She needs to be shaken gently, or stirred, even with the alarm radio on. Eyes left, I could see she still had a few dreams to go.

Should I go for my walk? I'll surely be back before Genna wakes. Need to be careful not to rehearse my answers. I'm going, I thought without much more hesitation. My morning walks put me in tune with the day. The days I skip, I don't think as clearly or calmly about events that come up. I sure do need my thoughts today to be calm and direct.

The peace and quiet of the still morning is a good time for my prayers. I realized a while ago that the Church needed to put out all of its trash, in its house and under the rugs, before it could expect to teach me how to be a better person. Since then, I've cut out the middleman, and prayed directly for goodness and guidance. I just offer prayers for specific friends and family, and also for the good, strife torn people. The prayers I use are contained in the rosary, but any other set of prayers can be used. This format can be used with any religion. It's nice to remember we owe Someone who put us here.

Set the house alarm, whooshed out the door, and onto the pavement of our gated community.

I finished my prayers, was back at the house, and feeling very ready to face the day.

"Get back to the Ark today!" suddenly echoed in my head, as if from earphones.

I grabbed the railing to steady myself. At this point, I was willing to bet the Ark door would be open.

Back to square one on the calmness front. I was a wreck, afraid to go back inside the house, to face Genna asking what was wrong. I gradually started to get a grip while sitting on the front stoop, and gained inspiration from the monarch butterfly on the huge, fragrant bush next to the front door. The beautiful creature bobbed and weaved deceptively from the light pink flowers, collecting nectar from each. I would be truthfully deceptive to Genna at breakfast. I opened the door, did my quick trick with the alarm, and headed toward Genna in the bedroom. The clock radio was already on, but Genna was still motionless. I gently shook her shoulder.

"Wake up, sleepy! What would you like for breakfast?"

Not much movement, but after a few groans, yawns, and eye rubs, she said, "Where were you last night?" as she struggled to sit upright.

"I stopped by the old Ark on the Sunnyside campus. I was on my way home, so I decided to reminisce about the old b-ball games I used to see there. Luckily, someone left a back door open, and I got inside. That Ark is still an amazing place. What would you like for breakfast?"

She'll never know HOW amazing. So far, so good. I wasn't lying, so I didn't feel like I was pressing. Also, it wasn't like I was trying to buy her off, I was the breakfast chef anyway.

"Bullshit. What do you mean; you went to the old 'Ark'? Please."

"Actually, a thousand dollar hooker jumped in the car at a light, and said the first time was free."

"No, really," I said. You know I'm more of a basketball junky than ever. It was cool." More like chilly, I thought. "Which story do you think is closer to the truth?" Perhaps, I overdid the contrast, I thought.

"You really stopped by the Ark?"

I guess my bob and weave worked, “Yes!” I said.

Trust is a very good thing. Also, Genna knows how seriously I took her threat to take a sharp knife to my privates while I slept, should I ever get caught in the latter scenario.

“Bacon, eggs, toast, coffee?”

“Sounds good,” she said. What are your plans today?”

“I have to get us a few groceries at Wagner’s Food Mart. Then, I want to go back to the Ark to see what it looks like during the daylight. I wonder what kind of things go on in this day and age. I’ve always liked the architectural design of the place, and it always seemed quite functional for a myriad of activities. I’m just wondering if it’s still being put to good use today as before.”

I realized I was talking on two different levels here, one for her, and one for me, and it seemed to be working.

“Take your shower while I’m making breakfast. I’ll have it on the table ten minutes after I hear the shower stop. How’s that?” That’s fine with me, I thought. The less Q and A with Genna this morning, the better.

“Ok. Sunnyside, please?”

For a split second, I was thinking about the alma mater.

“Coming right up.”

I could have made it as a short order cook. I have a knack for quickness and timing while plating a breakfast order. I know how long she takes to shower, and I had the dish ready 10 minutes after, as promised. Neither of us like to wait or eat cold eggs.

I ate fast, as usual, before Genna finished hers. There was only time for a bit of small talk, without any endearments.

“I’ll go to the Ark first, then Wagner’s. I should be back in a couple of hours,” as I headed for my shower.

"Take your time," Genna said. "On second thought, why don't I go to the Ark with you? I'll clean up, blow out my hair, and throw something on while you shower, then get dressed. It may be fun for me. too."

I wasn't ready for this curve ball.

"Gen, this time I'd like to see it by myself. I'd spent much more time there than you. We've only shared a couple of games and concerts. If you don't mind, I'd like to imagine the past today on my own. Soon, I'll take you there, if you want, but today I'd rather be alone with my thoughts."

I just flicked my wrists at her curve, and hit a single.

As I was saying this, I made haste toward my shower, in an attempt to cut off conversation all together.

"Ok. Maybe, when you get back, we can do something together?"

Whew!

"Sure. Think of something you might want to do."

I couldn't shit, shower, shave, and get dressed fast enough.

* * *

I was out of the garage in my Eos when I realized I forgot the shopping list. Screw it; I wasn't going back in the house to chance Genna throwing another question at me.

Rather than put the top down on this beautiful day in the driveway, I zipped around the corner to do it there. For the next thirty seconds, I felt like I was in the movie, "Transformers." I get a kick every time I do it. "Das Auto" translation to me means "neat car."

Five minutes after I'm on my way again, the phone rings in the car. It's Genna. Silly to think with cell phones I can avoid another question for her.

"You forgot the shopping list."

"I just realized that. I know pretty much what we need, however. I'll go slower down the aisles and do shelf recognition. Is there anything you'd like to add to the list?"

"Don't forget my Lean Cuisines."

Genna has been battling our mutual, slow creeping poundage over the years more than I have, with minimal success. What I mean is, I've gained as much weight also, but she's tried harder to take it off. She subscribes to the old adage, "You can never be too rich, or too thin," which we are neither. Lately, I've tried to cheerfully describe our silhouettes as "slightly Rubenesque," which doesn't always humor her, but which I think conveys a form of happiness. Enjoying good food is a happy meal to us.

"Will do, dear."

Well, I thought, confronting Genna without spilling the beans went better than I expected. It was time to get back to thinking about how I became, "the One," as Slick put it. Why me? I'm just an average John who enjoys the game, has never lost my school spirit, and never fallen off the bandwagon during the lean years of poor performance. I can't put my finger on anything I've done to put me in the category of Noah, or Mary, the mother of Christ, who both heard calls from above somewhere. However, just like them, I was being asked to do something largely on faith. I didn't know why, and I didn't feel like I won a lottery.

The last voice I heard said return to the Ark TODAY, not tonight. I was keeping my eye on the speedometer; I didn't want to pull a stunt like last night that would get me stopped. The way I was feeling, I didn't need to come across as suspicious, agitated, or saying something that would send me to the pokey.

Although it was summertime, Sunnyside never sleeps. There would be many people over at the Ark, milling around for a myriad of reasons. Slick did say that it didn't matter, to them. How was I going to carry on a conversation with him, while other 2011ers think I'm talking to myself?

I arrived at the Ark parking lot. Fortunately, it was a “free zone,” and I didn’t require a campus parking sticker. This thought never occurred to me the night before because the lot was empty. Today, there were quite a few cars, but plenty of spaces also.

I went up to the same door where I gained entry last night, and which Slick said to use, and it was locked. I paused and thought, I’ll go around to the front, where I saw someone enter as I drove around to the back lot.

I started to turn away when I heard the door lock click. Looking up, I saw Slick, as he appeared last night, same uniform and all.

“Hey, John.”

Chapter Three

"Slick, how did you know I'd be here at this time today?"

"I didn't. I was just hoping you'd come back ASAP. You turned out to be the person I'd been hoping to find here. I've had hopes and dreams, more so than the other guys on the team. We all love this place, but there's gotta be a reason we keep replaying these games over and over here. Don't get me wrong, we still love playing. This was the best time in our lives. There's a higher power making us do this over and over. I think Stephen Hawking is full of it. There must be a God."

I heard a voice this morning, out of nowhere, telling me to return to the Ark, today. Was that you?"

"Say what?" I can't say anything that can be heard outside this building, and inside, only to my team, and now, you. In fact, none of us can even LEAVE this place. I can't explain the voice. Take that again, Mr. Hawking!" Slick said.

"Hey Mister, are you alright? You're talking to yourself." A scruffy, back packed student in shorts and a blue Sunnyside tee shirt was staring at me out of the corner of his eye.

"Don't mind me," I fumbled. "Sometimes I mumble to myself… it's a long story," was the best I could manage. The kid just shrugged, and sauntered away from us.

Slick was getting a good laugh out of this. "Sorry, I forgot. Today, it's not just the watchman we have to consider while talking. I'll make sure no one's around when we talk," as we moved over to courtside. This could be a neat trick. There wasn't a game day crowd in the place, but enough to cause stares if I wasn't careful to whisper. "C'mon, the guys are waiting for me so we can play Mega again."

Sure enough, there was the Mega starting five getting ready for the jump ball, and the Sunnyside players minus Slick doing the same. Then I noticed something very strange, again. None of the Mega players seemed to be aware of my presence, yet the "Sunny" players all nodded my way.

"Slick, why can't the Mega players see me?"

"You mean nothing to them, or they to you. All of your energy is with us. How much, and what kind of energy, I don't know, but it enabled you to be here with us. I still don't have all the answers, we'll just have to let this all play out, and learn as we go."

"Slick, how often do you beat these guys?

"John, I said back then, after we played them in real time, we could probably win six or seven out of ten, and that pretty much has been the case. That first game, we weren't ready for the big stage." Slick then took his place on the court, and another five on five was about to begin. Ball up.

I stood on the sidelines, trying to absorb the surreal spectacle before me. On the court were the ten players and three referees. Across the court on the other sideline there were a few substitute players for each squad, and the head coach for each team. These other players and the coaches didn't seem to acknowledge my presence, except for "BB," the sixth man for Sunnyside. He gave me a thumb up from the far sideline. I guess Slick was right, I seemed as invisible to all but the six Sunny players as every player on the court did to the present day people milling around the Ark. Each player had a faint aura around him, not as intense or beacon like as the night before; I guessed because it was daytime.

The players exchanged gentle knuckle bumps in lieu of handshakes for good luck, took their places around the jump circle, oblivious to the

2011 students and staff members of the College who were walking right through them, going about their present day business.

This was short circuiting my mind watching two "realities" collide in the same space. It wasn't the past colliding with the present, exactly. The game, as Slick pointed out to me, was not just a replay; it had an outcome yet to be determined. So to them, and to me watching, this was real.

I spotted a newspaper left on a chair in the corner of the gym. I walked over to retrieve it, figuring to use it as a ruse to avert my eyes, instead of watching the imaginary (to everyone else in the present) game being played up and down the court. It was yesterday's, but it would have to do. I sauntered back to a sideline area near half court, glancing down at the newspaper, left to right at the court, around the gym to see who was staring at me, then back down to the print again. By the end of the day, I thought, I would find out if this was an eye strain or an exercise.

Before me, I was watching the game played the way that made me a rabid fan for life.

I like speed. Both of these teams played in overdrive the whole game. Also, the coaches let them play, just offering minor pointers, as did the refs, the three of them seeming to forget they had whistles. The other curious thing about the game was there were no dunks. Then I remembered there was a no dunking rule in place back then. What a lame rule, which they rescinded a few years later. The dunk is the home run of basketball. Half the tickets sold are probably to watch who dunks on whom. Despite the fact they were being allowed to play the way they wanted, there didn't seem to be much joy on their faces. They all seemed very businesslike, although it was clear both teams wanted to win.

I only remember a couple of players on the Mega team, one guard, and their center. Those were the players who killed us in the real game one. Their names escape me, but the guard was a half step faster than our Quincy Wilson, and the center got the best of our freshman center,

Johnny Bird. In today's rematch, Quincy and John had their numbers, and Sunny won by five points.

Hugs and pats on the head accompanied the final buzzer, as both teams headed towards their respective benches. There was no elation for the winners or sadness for the losers. It was like the outcome really didn't matter. It was like watching a looping tape replay over and over.

Slick came over to me, as the other players huddled around, waiting to hear what he and I had to say to each other.

"John, did you enjoy the game? Brought back old memories, didn't it?"

I folded the newspaper under my arm, caught Slick's gaze with mine, and head gestured to all the real people walking around us.

"I hear you. C'mon, there's a small supply room to the side of the locker room where no one ever goes. You can talk, or at least whisper to me."

I followed him to the door that leads to this room, but at the last second, I swooped ahead of him to open the door before he did, in case another real person was watching me. Instead of using the door, he walked through the wall instead. He was right. Inside, just a bunch of janitorial supplies, and no one seemed to be in ear shot. I would whisper anyway.

"Yes and no, Slick." I said. "I appreciated seeing the talent and skill you all had back then, but the joy and sorrow of winning and losing just isn't there. I really want to believe the game really happened before my eyes, but the lack of emotion made it all seem like a fake. Maybe I AM imagining all of this. I want to believe you that I'm here, and can see and hear all this, for a reason. I wasn't sent here to watch you guys play game after game without some sort of higher purpose."

"I hear you, John. The file in the Universe explanation, even if I didn't make it up, would only go so far. I did talk to the guys after you left last night. None of them was really wondering, as I was, why we keep doing this over and over. They just assumed this fragment of their lives was archived like a videotape which could be written over again and again. (I noticed he didn't say CD, or DVD, which weren't yet on the market). I convinced them there was more to it. I told them there must be a satisfaction or salvation which we haven't experienced that keeps us doomed in limbo. At least, until we figure this out, we've all continued to be here for each other, just like the old days. John, each one of them wants to talk to you. If we can figure out why it was you, John, who showed up, and not someone else, it may help us to understand why this is all still happening."

Suddenly, I realized I'd been at the Ark for almost an hour and a half. Genna's going to wonder why I spent so much time here. I'd better leave now. I can fake traffic on Route 20, get down to Wagner's, whiz through the aisles, hoping not to forget much that is on the list I forgot to take with me.

"Slick, I need to leave here now. I've got errands to do today, in 2011, and my wife wants me to take her out this afternoon. I told her I was coming here today to reminisce. That, to her, should take a few minutes. I'll get back here as soon as I can, with an excuse that will let me spend more time with you and the guys. I won't let any of you down. Together, we'll get to the bottom of this. Who wants to talk to me first when I come back?"

"Charlie."

With Slick, I could see the Sunny six heading off to the showers, after we said our goodbyes. Today, it was just a few waves; I was really pressed for time. Again, as I got into the Eos, I had this queasy feeling that I was in two different time zones, sort of like jet lag. I took care behind the wheel; I didn't need an accident, or to get stopped for any other reason.

* * *

Shit. There really was traffic on Route 20. I was just about to turn on the excuse mobile when the cars started moving again. A car had a flat tire in the left lane, and needed to get to the right shoulder.

Wagner's wasn't too crowded, which was very unusual. I maneuvered each aisle, taking optical snapshots of items on the shelves that we were missing, and needed at home. Yes, I remembered the Lean Cuisines.

The phone rang out of the dash in the Eos. I pressed the receive button without needing to look at the caller ID.

"Where are you?" Genna said. Actually, I expected her call a lot sooner.

"I'm just leaving Wagner's parking lot. When I got to the Ark, there was a basketball game with some old timers. I don't think you'd remember any of them, but some of them could still play pretty well. I lost track of time; you know what a sucker I am for a good game. Also, there was traffic on Route 20 going to Wagner's."

I didn't lie.

"It's not too hot, so I'd like to go over to Red Shoals, stroll around, grab a bite at Baruta's, then look at a couple of condos for our consideration a few years from now."

Genna could always get me to tag along doing what she, not I, really wanted to do, by throwing me a bone, so to speak. Actually, it was a meatball this time. When she mentioned Baruta's, I started to salivate, thinking of a light lunch with my customary side order. Their Italian meatball has just the right combo of beef, pork, and veal, and with their homemade sauce, they're addictive. I often order another portion to take home.

They're that good.

Just the walking around and looking at condos was not going to do it for me, and she knew it. She loves to window shop and get decorating ideas from open houses, both of which I hate. But, a promise is a promise.

Don't get me wrong about Red Shoals. It's a pretty town with lots to do, twenty-five or so Zagat rated eateries, great views of the Nemacole River, and only a half hour from our home in Marlton. The river is "brackish," a mixture of salt and fresh water, and a high iron content gives it a slightly rust color, probably giving Red Shoals its name.

I returned home with the groceries to see that surprise, surprise, Genna was ready to go. This is an extremely rare feat for her. We never arrive anywhere on time. I've made the excuse time and again to friends that Genna's philosophy is to blame. To her, in theory, being late she will never die; she'll miss her own funeral.

She even helped me stock the provisions I just purchased. I really must be dreaming. We locked the house, plopped into the Eos, and headed for Red Shoals, Baruta's for sure.

We hit Baruta's just right; the business lunchers had already left. The bushels of tomatoes are abundant near the front entrance; each tomato picture perfect, and ready to become their near perfect sauce in a few days' time. We both ordered a pint of their seasonal beers from the microbrewery on site. Genna's a soup head, so she ordered the pasta fagioli, which is a meal in itself. Veal Parmegian with the meatball side did it for me.

From home and driving to the restaurant, Genna barely said a word. I thought she might not be feeling well. Besides this possibility, her quietude could mean a number of things. She's getting ready to pepper me with questions about my time this morning, not believing that I watched an old timer's game. Or, she could be getting ready to ask me for something, which is usually her reason for asking to do something together.

"What a gorgeous day to be out and about," she said.

Small talk. This was good. No "John, I've been meaning to ask..." I began to think that she really didn't want anything besides my company.

"It's terrific, eighty degrees and low humidity, not the typical early July scorcher. We'll go anywhere your heart desires, sugar. It'll be good to walk off lunch."

With that remark, lunch was served. We always share a little of each dish, with the lion's share still going to the one who ordered the portion. Genna rattled off a walking itinerary which involved a couple of art galleries we hadn't seen in a while, as well as passing through the antique district, where reasonable prices are the general rule.

"Then I'd like to see two condos in a building by the Nemacole, just to get the feel of the building, and how it's maintained, for future reference."

This trip seemed potentially inexpensive. We are basically "observant" gallery goers, as opposed to "purchasers." The antique stores provide us with small memento-like gifts, such as an old tea service for one. The Visa card may not make it out of my wallet.

The meal was first rate, as always. The waiter brought the check when I heard someone as near as he say, as clear as day, this:

"Charlie needs to talk tonight."

I glanced up at the waiter, who was silent. He said nothing, just dropped off the check. Genna was rummaging through her purse. She heard nothing.

The sound I heard this morning was as clear, as close by, and I was by myself. It was also clear to me now that I am alone in this; not Genna and I, just me.

"Charlie needs to talk, TONIGHT."

The voice had a sense of urgency. How the hell am I going to spring myself later?

"John, are you alright?" as she looked up from her mini carpet bag of a purse.

"I'm fine. I was just thinking, after we're finished this afternoon, I'll make us a light supper, and then I might head over to the campus book-store that's across from the old Ark. I was going to stop this afternoon, but I lost track of time. There having a sale on Sunny memorabilia, tee shirts, and the like. Want to come?"

I didn't expect her to say yes, Genna is not a triathlete when it comes to stamina, and we were about to pace a good part of the town. I cashed out our tab, and gave our waiter a generous tip. I have a soft spot for the struggling, student-type waiter.

"I'll see how I feel after we see the condo."

Not what I expected, but I was still willing to bet she'd be too tired.

* * *

Red Shoals is a diverse town with lower middle, to upper class income, and a variety of retail businesses to take care of that range. It borders Ryeburg, which you'll encounter if you continue east along Front St. as it becomes River Rd. There's a lot of coin in that town. Most homes have great views of the river and the Atlantic Ocean, and are giant metaphors for cash registers, cha ching!

We walked from Baruta's toward Main St, which forms a T with Front St. Main St, for a few blocks is almost Fifth Ave. in New York City; high fashion and pricy apparel, before the offerings become more reasonable. It doesn't matter to Genna; she looks for ideas, not prices. She's great at finding knock-offs of shoes, clothing, and accessories she's seen in high end stores, for a shoe string price. Genna's in her glory, while I'm feigning interest. I'm happier when she walks inside a women's store, and I stay outside, parked on a nearby bench, waiting and hoping she reappears without a package.

The next few hours melt away . We cover about twenty blocks while working our way over to the condo building near the Nemacole River, where two units have open houses. Both of the units are on the 6th floor, just the right height to form a perfect view of the boats, docks, and riverside cabanas. I've never understood why people want to be as high up in such a building as possible. All you view is the sky. You miss the flavor of the area. Both units were nice, very nice. One needed a little work, but what a view! I thought to myself, I could live here in the future for six months, then our place in Florida the other six.

It turns out the building is actually a co-op, and as we were leaving a few of the owners gave us their own personal sales pitch; full occupancy lowers their costs.

"I think I'll skip the bookstore," Genna said predictably. "You don't have to make supper; I'll just have a Lean Cuisine." After Wagner's, plenty of those to choose from, I thought.

"Fine. There are a couple of slices of pizza left. They'll do for me." Anything quick, I thought, to get me back over to the Ark.

We returned to Baruta's parking lot where we left the car, dropped the small "thinking of you" gift for our future daughter-in-law in the back seat, started the engine, and headed back to Marlton. Genna was asleep in less than a mile, a by-product, I think, of her parents putting her in the car as a toddler, and driving her around the block to meet the sandman.

At home, four minutes in the microwave for hers, five minutes in the oven (I can't stand soggy left over pizza) for mine. Ten minutes to eat, gargle, and zip back to the Ark to see Charlie.

Charlie

It was around six o'clock when I hit the traffic mess that occurs where Route 5 meets Route 20. The bookstore was open until 8PM, so I had time. How was I going to make it seem I was at the book store for an hour and a half? Genna knows I hate to shop. She knows my idea of shopping is opening a catalogue or surfing Amazon.com. I was going to have to wing it. I parked the car behind the Ark, raced around the building and across Colters Ave. to the bookstore. There was an overwhelming selection of apparel and trinkets; almost anything they could stamp a Sunnyside logo on. I grabbed two run of the mill tee shirts, one white on blue, one blue on white (school colors, remember), paid, and raced back over to the car to throw the shirts in the trunk.

I looked at my watch. I had about an hour before Genna's predictable phone call.

There were fewer cars in the lot than I expected. I guessed during the summer, most of the business in the Ark occurred during the day. The door was open anyway, but there wasn't one of my spirits to greet me. A few students were milling around, walking across the court. I made haste toward that supply room that Slick showed me, opened the door, and there was Charlie Bennett in his clean, blue on white home uniform, circa 1971.

"Hi, John. Slick seems to think you can help us."

Before me stood the legend himself. I had never met him back in 1971, but I did meet him a few times over the years since, at banquets and Back Court functions, the booster club of which I was a member. He was not the person standing before me now. He was always gracious to old fans such as me who acknowledged his accomplishments, but he sure didn't seem happy in general. Here he was before me, in his prime, chiseled like a statue of David, yet to show his first ounce of fat, with a short trimmed beard...

His eyes gave him away. No smirk or half smile could take away their sadness. Those eyes weren't happy reliving his glory days.

"Charlie, I hope I can help you first."

He looked at me with hope. I felt badly that I hadn't a clue yet how to go about helping any of them. I thought it might be significant that CB asked to see me first. Knowing what happened to each of them 40 years into the future, I knew Charlie, for having the most success on the team, fared most poorly in later life.

Looking for someplace to start, I said, "Charlie, there's got to be a connection between your past, how you're feeling now, in 1971, and what has happened to you leading up to the real present."

"I just feel like what we accomplished as a team didn't matter. We went to the Championship, man." Charlie's head drooped and his eyes gazed at the floor. The Final Four in the NCAA tournament is the cocktail hour before the reception. It's an affirmation that your team belongs among the best, has been invited, and has arrived. The Championship means you're vying for the lion's share of the moneybag full of envelopes.

"It's like we got this far, I got them this far, we laid the foundation, but the house was never built. This place is not a refuge, but an asylum, and we're going crazy. Me and my teammates are stuck here, getting erased and replayed over and over again. Why Mega U, why do we keep playing Mega? Slick is right. This all has to have a purpose." CB glanced up at me, before staring at the floor again. He looked embarrassed. "John, I know I f****d up after my playing days. I put all my apples into basketball. It was all I was really good at, and I let everything else slide, or did just what I had to, so I could keep playing ball. I only had one dream, John. I should have had two, one to fall back on."

"Charlie, I'm sorry to see you feeling this way. These should be happy memories. They were the best time of your life. You carved out a memorable place in history for quite a few people. Most of us can only rely on our family to remember us, and some don't even have that. Despite the way you feel, you've done something very special. You're still Charlie Bennett, and what you did still means something. It's like you sent a gift that was lost in transit. I'm hoping it can still be delivered. Maybe that's why I'm here."

I seemed to get CB's attention. He straightened up, squared his head, neck and shoulders, and gazed at me with a glimmer of hope.

"I need to go now, but I'll be back to talk with the other guys, to see how they fit into this puzzle. I agree with you about having two dreams, but maybe your one was still enough. That one dream of yours made a lot of people dream they were you!" I wanted to leave Charlie on a high note. I wanted to leave with that glimmer of hope in his eye becoming an ember, where his fire used to be.

"Charlie, the other thing I want you to know is a voice is guiding me through this. Like today, I heard, as clear as day, that you needed to talk to me. I come here, and you, just you are waiting for me. It's like Someone or Something wants me to solve this. It gives ME hope."

We shook hands, and CB seemed a bit happier, and more trustful of me than when we first met.

I got in the car, and decided to preempt Genna giving her a call. The line was busy. A few seconds later, my phone rings. Genna is calling.

"I'm on my way home, sugar." After forty years together, this happens a lot.

Chapter Four

It was a little after 8 P.M. and the sun was turning red toward the western horizon. There were wispy red cirrus clouds forming a crown around the setting sun. The old nautical adage came to mind. "Red sky at night, sailor's delight" had been taught to me as a kid by my old salt grandfather. I didn't really have a chance to appreciate this painted sky because the traffic was moving, and I didn't want to be on the losing side of a rear ender. Besides, I had that twilight feeling again, living in two different worlds. This masterpiece of Nature would seep into the darkness in a half hour, by the time I got home.

I wouldn't be surprised if Genna took a nap after supper, and might still be snoozing when I arrived. I quietly entered the house, did my quick alarm trick, and then tiptoed into the dark house. I could not see, but I heard:

"Hello. Red Shoals really wiped me out. I'm just resting my eyes in the wing chair. What did you get at the bookstore?"

"A couple of tee shirts that you just reminded me are still in the car. I'm going back out to get them." In the garage, I popped the trunk, and heard that voice again.

"Quincy's next."

At this point, I didn't get any chills or weak knees. However, I didn't think Quincy Wilson would be the next of the players wanting to talk to me. He had the most success after his college days of any of them. As much of a problem for helping to solve this mystery, was how I was going to arrange more frequent trips to the Ark, without seeming strange to Genna. So far, I'd been able to finesse my excuses with elements of truth. Genna and I had agreed long ago never to lie to each other, fib, maybe, but not lie.

Returning to the house, I showed Genna my purchases. She was unimpressed.

"Genna, it was all very confusing (true). They had so much stuff; I really couldn't decide what I really wanted. Tee shirts always come in handy for me (half truth)." She accepted this, knowing what a lousy shopper I am.

I turned on a small background light to lessen the eyestrain from the TV, which I turned on next. Flipping channels, I found some news to snooze by, mostly about upbeat, human interest stories, rather than the misanthropic deeds the dregs of the world are involved with. After a half hour, the busy day was catching up with me also. The twilight feeling was drifting toward sleep. What to do about tomorrow, and an excuse to get back to the Ark. Genna was already in snooze mode when I clicked off the TV. Easing my head onto the pillow, I chuckled as I thought of Meatloaf, the singer:

"Baby, baby, let me sleep on it. Let me sleep on it, I'll give you an answer in the morning …"

* * *

The sunlight in the room had me guess the time as about 6:30AM. A glance over at the clock radio said 6:19. Another glance at Genna lying next to me made me wonder again how she stays asleep being a nocturnal contortionist. Her left arm was over her head on the pillow, her head turned left at me, her right leg hanging off the bed below the knee, and her other leg folded together. She sure seems like an active dreamer, although she says she isn't. I hope she doesn't dream about kicking me.

I slowly slid off the bed to my feet, slipped into my walking attire, and tread lightly towards my bathroom, avoiding as many loose floor boards as I could remember. I proceeded with my morning hygienic routine, the details of which I'll spare you. After retrieving the morning papers outside, I retreated to the kitchen refrigerator to get an idea for breakfast. Oatmeal, I thought, to unclog a few arteries. I opened the breakfast island drawer to check the calendar for today's agenda.

Oh, good. Genna's got a haircut scheduled for late morning. After that, she'll probably resort to her favorite compulsion, window shopping. I'll probably be able to get lost for about two hours.

Reopening the fridge, I served myself a few prunes, a probiotic pill, and a glass of water. That combo along with my daily walk keeps me a regular guy, so to speak. I'm out the door into the development, which is still a work in progress. I hear the air driven nailers and back hoes working on a house about two blocks away from ours. Genna can sleep through these sounds. Luckily, I'm an earlier riser, because I cannot.

Briskly again, like yesterday, heal, toe, and prayers, for forty five minutes.

Returning home, I quietly re-enter the house. I hear the clock radio on, which means Genna's in the process of waking. Going directly into the kitchen, I glean the papers to see what else is wrong with the world. I don't want to come off as a pessimist; I'm really not. The world just seems to be trending that way lately. Now that my body is awake, I need to do the same for my mind, and the crossword puzzle usually does the trick. The current events can wait, since I most likely saw then already on TV or the internet. After my best stab at the crossword, the local events in the paper get my attention.

Genna sleepily trod into the kitchen, gave me a rainbow wave with a 90 degree elbow, and a kiss on the cheek.

"Oatmeal?"

"Sure," she says.

"How did you sleep?"

"OK, but John, you were talking in your sleep. Something about ... "Charlie ... don't worry." There was more, but I was still half asleep myself."

I feigned a quizzical look, and said, "Really. I don't remember any of that (a fib). You don't remember anything else I said?"

"No. Like I said, I was still asleep."

That was a relief. I begin to wonder at what point I'm going to spill the beans to her. Please, I hope not. I continue to wonder about this as I'm making the oatmeal, not too soupy, not too dry. When it's ready, I spoon it into separate bowls; then she does her thing to hers, and I do mine. I add granola with dried fruit, a half a banana, flaxseed, and vanilla soy milk. Breakfast of champions. I'll spare you what she does with hers. A cup of green tea does it for me, to accompany her cup of coffee.

As we're eating, I ask her, "Have I been talking in my sleep lately, the last couple of nights?"

"Not that I can recall, besides those few words last night. By the way, I'm getting my haircut later this morning, so I better hit the shower. What are your plans?"

"I don't know yet, exactly. I'll put together a few errands while you're gone, I'm sure."

She was off to the shower before proceeding into her "get ready" mode, which to me is akin to a moon shot countdown.

After rinsing the dishes for her to clean up later, I decided to piddle around in my English flower garden at the front of the house. This is my little piece of heaven on the property. It's just as much as I want to do in the way of gardening these days; a half hour a day is usually all that's required. There's a mixture of evergreen shrubs and perennial flowers in a semi-shade/sunny area that's on either side of the walkway to the front entrance. Actually, our "front" entrance is on the side of the house, so we have two wide side beds along the walk leading up to the entrance steps. The pink azaleas, boxwood, and burning bushes are interspersed with the dense perennials, including multicolored daylilies, pink and white astilbes, multicolored irises, coneflowers, black eyed susans, clematis, and columbines among assorted wildflowers, most of whose names escape me. The pink dogwood on the corner leads up to two giant light pink butterfly bushes, which seem to supply most of the nectar for the butterflies and hummingbirds in the county. I went over to stand on the side of my neighbor Mike's driveway about twenty feet away, which offers the best view around the corners of my little Eden. I've asked him, and have been granted, "gazing rights" to view my garden from that spot.

"Are you going to see Quincy today?" That voice again.

This threw me a bit. A QUESTION?

I looked around. The voice seemed to come from all directions. It wasn't loud; it just had an enveloping quality to it.

I looked around, again, to see if anyone could listen.

"Yes," I whispered.

"Good."

I went back to the garden to try to do what I came out to do, pick those few weeds that were trying to make a go of it amongst the dense foliage. I was shaking. I managed to fumble on weeding for the ten minutes it took. The plants were given a good drink of water while I thought of getting a good shot of vodka.

I returned inside the house, and got a sugar cookie instead, which seemed to do the trick of calming me down. Genna strode into the kitchen, ready to go. Record time, I thought, but I remembered she didn't have to fuss with her hair today.

"I'll be home by mid afternoon;" Just as I thought.

After a kiss on my cheek, she was into the car in the garage. Door up, door down, away she went.

After a record time shower and change, I was driving to the Ark. I'd think of the errands later.

Quincy

Here it was midmorning, and I was having that twilight feeling again. It's like all the molecules in my body are readjusting to the unknown zone I'll be subjecting them to. I'm not fearful. I'm sort of used to it happening at this point. Maybe I watched too many Star Trek episodes, but I start thinking that this must have been the feeling the members of the *Starship Enterprise* felt as they were about to be "beamed up."

I again start speculating why Quincy Wilson would be the second to want to talk to me. As I said, he's been the most successful of all his teammates after he left the hardwood of Sunnyside . His family was extremely wealthy, and he didn't have to bounce a ball after Sunny-side. He could just manage the family portfolio and cash those dividend checks, but bouncing that ball was his first love. The money for him would always be there. I'm trying to think what may have happened after his college playing days that left him unfulfilled, and tormented by something that might have been.

Quincy, as a reminder, was the point guard of the team. I can make an argument with anyone for at least fifteen minutes that the name of the game should be "Point Guard," not basketball. The point guard is a combination spark plug and thyroid gland that controls the speed or tempo of the game. He calls out the plays, constantly monitoring what the other team's defense will allow him to do. He's the coach on the floor. His success depends on how he can direct his teammates into position for the highest percentage shot at the basket. There's a lot of finesse involved in being a good point guard. The other players must be kept happy, and get their share of "touches" with the basketball. A great point guard can turn around a team's fortune noticeably in one year. If football is a game of inches, as a great coach once said, then basketball is a game of split seconds, and those rapid decisions are made by the point guard.

Quincy was a great point guard. With all he was responsible for on the court, his knowledge exceeded the other players. That knowledge served him well in the professional ranks, where he had a solid, if not stellar career, while managing to win a championship ring for his efforts. Professional players make a lot of money, (which didn't faze Q anyway), but it's the ring, ala Tolkien, that binds their pursuit. Quincy's knowledge took him further as a successful pro coach, and, to this day, he's still at it.

So again, why, is he involved in this futile endeavor?

I kept looping this around in my head all the way to the Ark, which traffic-wise was uneventful. The Eos seemed to know the way by now; I was parked and heading for the back door in no time.

The court area was being covered with folding chairs lengthwise across, with a raised dais and speaker's lectern facing the rows and rows of sky blue and white seats. I had a flashback to my freshman assembly I've told you about, happily recalling that I was one of the two that made it. I was also glad to see the guys weren't playing amongst the chairs; that would have amounted to a terrible headache for me.

Off to the supply room where I expected to find Q, and I did. The same deal as Charlie, uniform wise, and "Quick" had his mop head haircut circa 1971, which waved to either side of his head as he sped down court.

"Q, you're the only one on this team who I haven't ever met, even in future years." I realized how strange that sounded, but it didn't seem to faze him.

"John, it's nice to finally meet you, then, even under these circumstances."

"I wonder, Quincy, if I'll ever get to meet you in real time."

"One never knows. I think I'd like that though, based on the talk I had with CB. I haven't seen him look and feel this good in all these years. You said something to him that did him a whole lot of good. He even played a lot better last night, after you had your talk. He knocked down forty points."

“I’m glad to hear he’s feeling better. All I did was offer encouragement that I could figure this out. I also told him that despite things not working out the way he’s planned, he still made a big difference in the memory bank of a lot of people.”

“That’s what I thought, but Charlie kept the conversation to himself. That’s CB. He just said the talk you had was good, and I can see on the court that it was.”

“Q, what do you think is going on here? You went on to bigger and better things. You were and are very successful. How much of your real self forty years from now, knows and feels what’s going on here?”

“I think of these days every now and then, but not nearly as much as Charlie. I talk to him in real time every month or so, and he says he thinks about these days all the time. I’m not going to speak for the other guys because you haven’t talked to them yet.”

This may be significant, I thought. But why is Q still here as much as the other guys, being subject to the same loop in time? Individual regret didn’t seem to have much to do with it. Some collective force kept them all here regardless of what happened to them since.

“Q, all you guys do is keep replaying Megamont, correct?”

“Yes.”

“Why do you think that is? For forty years, you keep playing the same team over and over: Mega. Do you talk to their players? What do they think is going on?”

‘You know, John, it’s strange. We don’t talk to each other. In the real first game, we tried some small talk, but they wouldn’t say anything. We could tell they thought they were better than us and were trying to psych us out. Obviously, they were successful; we didn’t show up that day. In these replays, we don’t even bother anymore. They still play hard, and they always want to win, but that’s all they do is play. After the game, they just walk off, no hugs or shakes. They’re like ghosts of ghosts! It's like we're imagining them to be there to help us do what we've gotta do."

Ghosts of ghosts, I thought, just when I thought this couldn't get any stranger.

"Quincy, can you tell anything about their demeanor? I mean, do they seem more content than the Sunny players, like, this doesn't matter because we won the real one?"

"John, now that you mention it, yeah, like they think this is a good way to stay in shape. It's like they're doing us a favor in their spare time, while to us it's a job."

"Q, you've been a big help. I think I'm getting a much better handle on this. I've got to go now, before I'm missed. I haven't told anyone else about our meetings; although I'm not sure they could help. However, I don't want to end up in a psych ward, and be of no use to any of you. Let me ask you one more question before I go. Does it bother the team that next to nothing was said about the fortieth anniversary of your accomplishment during this past season by the Athletic Department?"

"A lot."

Two words were all Quincy said. His gaze at the floor offered the same lament as CB had the day before, and spoke volumes more than his answer.

Chapter Five

Ken Blarney is President of the Back Court, which is a collection of the rest of us fanatics who would like nothing better than to see college basketball games all year round. His knowledge of all things Sunny basketball has given him the nickname (by me) of “the Seer”. In keeping with our thirst for basketball year round, I would be seeing him at the Summer League in Bella Vista, DE, a popular shore town a half hour the other way from my house. I didn’t plan it this way, but it is convenient to have all my live basketball a half hour from my house.

The Summer League roster is an amalgam of players there for a variety of reasons. Some are professionals staying in shape during the off season, others are overweight has-beens with the strongest knee braces possible. There are freshman recruits coming into the various programs in the area, as well as currently enrolled players at those schools. Our team was almost the entire recruiting class plus two current players on one roster. It’s a great chance for a basketball junkie to get a first look at our upgraded team for the new season.

I thought on my way home from the Ark, I would broach the subject of the fortieth anniversary with Ken at the game that night.

First, before returning home, I had to zip through the errands I concocted to cover my time before Genna’s midafternoon queries about my time spent.

I arrived at Honey’s Cleaners without my laundry ticket in my haste to get to the Ark. It didn’t matter because I could just sign her copy.

However, what did matter would be Genna asking why I didn't take the old clothes. I forgot.

Honey's Cleaners is a mom and pop operation run by Honey, and her husband, Jack. They're both very sweet first generation Asian Americans whom I never bothered to ask their given names. They do very good work, never missing a crease, wrinkle, or spot. They both know my passion for Sunny basketball.

"John, you miss basketball?"

"No Jack, it never stops," as I explain the shore summer league. They both laugh at this crazy customer. Non-fanatics just don't understand.

I signed their receipt copy, smiled at being the joke to them, and then headed off to Lowe's for some plant fertilizer.

At Lowe's I walk the aisles scanning like my trip to Wagner's to see if anything else registers a need. Actually, I'm just killing time to appease my inquisitor, Genna.

Last stop, the liquor store, to get a bottle of Bombay Sapphire gin; which makes me, by a vote of one, the best martini in the world. I prefer the way I make them so much, I stopped ordering them out.

Genna's home when I return. She's happy to see me, and I'm happy to see no new packages from her. While we were still engaged, I saw Genna's shoe closet which resembled a scaled down version of a Nordstrom department. I credit blind true love for not taking that as a harbinger of her shopping capacity.

She probably was happy to see me, but seeing the gin bottle in the package I was carrying actually put the smile on her face.

"Cocktail time?" she asked.

"Can we stick with a glass of wine tonight? I'm going to a game with Calvin, and I'm driving. I'll throw a couple of steaks on the grill, broil some tater tots, wok the string beans, and uncork that bottle of riserva

Chianti. There's a little leftover garlic tomato sauce for the beans; what do you think?"

"As long as you're cooking,"

Genna is a very good cook, when she wants to be. However, she needs a recipe, which she'll execute to perfection, using level measuring spoons and all. My cooking is gene driven, from my Florentine grandmother, who was sponsored into this country as a cook for a wealthy Italian sportsman with houses in Bar Harbor, ME, New York City (today, the house is a national landmark), and Palm Beach, FL. Nana, as I called her, was an intuitive cook; no measuring, a sense of what would go well with whatever. She passed this on to my mother and me. Grilled steak originated in Florence ("bistecca fiorentina"). Anyway, I had everything prepped and delivered to the table in about forty minutes.

"I need a steak once every ten days or so," Genna said, "I don't care what the doctor says."

"I agree," and that's about what we do.

"John, you make a mean steak dinner."

"Well, I'm glad I can put all my energy into cooking the meal, since I don't have to clean up."

The sideward, under eye glance from her amounted to a sarcastic "ha ha," but she knew the deal; whoever doesn't cook, cleans up.

With that, I got up from the table and went upstairs to check my email account. Sure enough, one was from Calvin, confirming my 6:15 P.M. pick up at his house.

Brushed my teeth, gargled, changed into my Sunny tee and hat, and went to the kitchen where Genna was clanking the dishes to soak in the sink.

Gave her a "By, sugar," with a smooch on the cheek.

"If Calvin's wife has any interest, maybe the four of us can catch another game soon?"

"I'll ask."

I was rolling in the Eos at 6:10; I'd be on time. That's how closely we live to each other. During those five minutes, I began mulling the idea of mentioning to Calvin what was going on at the Ark. Cal and I have had a few conversations about our interests, and from the get-go he described himself as being a very spiritual person.

"I feel spiritual energy every day. Sometimes, my wife and friends think I'm crazy, but I'm not. There are forces out there which we haven't even begun to understand. There's a connectivity we can observe in other species that we can't observe in ourselves, at least not yet."

Essentially, Cal and I are on the same page with this, especially the part about "spiritual energy" everyday. If he only knew.

Should he know about the Ark? I decided not to pull that trigger just yet. It is interesting to me that Cal is a Jew, and I'm a Christian; both of us have probably lapsed more than our respective religious elders would like, yet we've reached a common spirituality outside our respective faiths.

As I said, I still pray to the principals of my faith, without needing the guidance of their current espousers. Heaven, I believe, is somewhere else in the universe, and whether I say God or Nature doesn't matter to me. Fellow travelers from 'There' who were on a higher plane of being could have come here, done the things that were recorded, and given the names we worship. I can deal with the semantic difference between God and Nature; some people can't.

Take that, Stephen Hawking!

Calvin, I think, has come to the same conclusion, except from the other side of the mountain. I believe what he says about connectivity. How else do a flock of starlings, or a school of fish, thousands each of them, turn on a dime at once?

"Hi, John," Cal said as I pulled up to his house.

I was deep in this thought, so the Eos almost drove itself to his house.

"I put the top down so you could fit your ex-cager frame into the seat with enough head room."

"I've had two WVs before, and always had plenty of head room," he said.

"Just to be sure."

I looked over and noticed that his head was pretty close to the airfoil, but he has thick, dirty blond/gray hair which should suffice to keep his hat on.

"Pick a satellite radio station," I said.

"The 60's would be good."

I hit the touch screen button for the 60's as I said, "You've got it."

"Little Deuce Coupe" by the Beach Boys started blaring out the dash. The Eos actually has a back seat, but only Lilliputians can fit there. We were off to the Shore League in Bella Vista.

The conversation started about the subject at hand, summer basketball, that is. The team had never really played together before. A couple of kids were from the DC-Baltimore area, a couple from NYC, from NJ, etc. They all know of each other; kids at that level of play know who's good, and who isn't. However, even in this first game, they were gelling, that is, starting to intuit their spacing on the court, and where best to be to score.

We both agreed with this assessment, and didn't bother to discuss the defense, which is notoriously absent during Summer League play. The coach will straighten that out on day one when formal practice begins in the fall.

We were almost at the end of Route 20. A couple of minor roads and side streets and we'd be at St. Mary's High School gym where the games were played. I was about to change the subject, but before I could speak,

"Tell NO ONE else!"

I swerved the car slightly, but enough to give Cal a start. He looked over at me and fidgeted in the seat. It was a good thing the top was down, for his head's sake.

"I'm OK. I thought I saw a piece of glass on the road (fib). Sorry, Cal."

A half a block away, on the corner from the gym, is a decent pizzeria, Focaccio's.

"Cal, Genna wants to know if your wife, Phyllis, would join us for a slice, then an upcoming game."

"That would be great, I'm sure. It'll have to wait until we get back from a cruise to Bermuda next week."

I looked at him from the corner of my eye, and said, "What kind of spirituality do you expect to find in the triangle? You're not going through the middle, I hope," I said kiddingly.

"Nah, were leaving from Bayonne (NJ)."

We parked the car a few blocks from the gym. By that time, calmness had returned to me. I had forgotten about the voices. I wish who or whatever would give me a sign; a little thunder, a gust of wind, clear the throat, something, and please don't do it in the car again?

As we got out of the car, I said to Cal," Is it me, or did the Athletic Department forget to acknowledge the fortieth anniversary of the Championship Final team?"

"Holy shit! You're right. I remember the team being honored every ten years. I remember a half time ceremony for the 10th, and every ten years after that. This isn't right."

"I agree," I said. "I'm going to speak to Ken Blarney if he's at the game tonight. He's the new president of the Back Court, you know. Maybe he can get the AD (Athletic Director) to do something the beginning of the upcoming season. It'll still be 2011, forty years later."

"Good Idea," Cal said. As I mentioned, Cal was a former journeyman college player, and did manage to get a tryout with a pro team. So, all in all, he was pretty good in his day, but I glanced at him striding towards the gym entrance favoring each knee, the consequence of too many rebounds. I'm sure he wished he had today's cushioned athletic footwear back in his playing days.

We headed up the steps and into St. Mary's High School gym on 9th Ave. in Bella Vista. It's a cozy place with fan seating on just one side, and team seating on the other. It seems not to have walls: instead, school banners and pennants cover every square inch of side space. The seats are made of the hardest plastic known to man. My theory is that an Archbishop designed them for penance, or prayers of forgiveness, to discourage future sinning.

We saw Ken, and his wife, June, at their front row seats, where, if you stretch your legs, your feet are in bounds.

"Do you like what you see, so far?" I asked Ken.

"I can't wait for the season," he replied.

Coming from Ken, this is his stock reply. No exclamation point. He's a certified fan for life. Good team, bad team, good coach, bad coach, he's there to offer his support. Cal and I know better, even if Ken won't get off his even keel. This year is going to be different.

"Ken, Cal and I were just saying that the AD never recognized the fortieth anniversary of the Champ Final team, and we don't think that's right. Has the Back Court broached the subject?"

"John, it has been brought up. This new coach wants to establish his own tradition. He wants his teams to be the dawn of a new day for Sunny Basketball. There is no past for him. It's this day forward, period."

Cal and I just looked at each other, astonished. Ken had a "just the messenger" look on his face.

I was deeply disappointed. I really liked this new coach. He is young. He is a coach's son, which gives him a leg up on everyone. He assembled a great coaching staff, deeply plugged into the NY and Philly metro area, and put together a first recruiting class second to few in the country. I wanted him to succeed, and stay a long time, but not on the backs of our history. So it is without championships, but these player alums were a great part of our college experiences, and they still deserved acknowledgement, and respect.

"Ken, that won't do, and you know it. He can't just build a moat around his program. These player alums can help his progress; they can be his ambassadors to anything from recruiting to financial support. We've got to try to change this attitude."

Calvin was nodding at the key words and commas of my argument.

"Now," I said, "the vague answer he gave me when I asked a related question at a Back Court meeting last year makes sense. I'm really serious about changing his mind on this, Ken. I'd be willing to draft a letter to him on your behalf. What say you?"

"Let me give it some thought. We may get some traction with it if we link it to a function of the club, that is, we in the Back Court could be doing this job for them."

"I agree," Cal said, "Saying we'll do it, instead of asking them to do it stands a better chance."

"Enough said, for now. Let's enjoy the game," I said.

I watched the game, but wasn't really taking it in. I began to mull the possibility that this situation with the new coach had something to do with my time at the Ark. The more I thought, the more convinced I was that it did, but why ME?

* * *

After the game, Cal and I said our goodbyes to Ken and June, and each pair headed off to their respective cars. Attending these summer games was further testament to Ken's and June's dedication, as they had well over an hour-and-a-half drive to get home versus our thirty minutes.

“What did you think?” asked Cal, as we approached the Eos. They’re really starting to gel. The spacing is much better, as is the intuition between players. You can tell these guys all have great court sense; it’s just a matter of learning each other’s preferences, strengths and weaknesses. I’m even more encouraged about our prospects this year.”

“I’m encouraged also, but I’m going to leave the jury out until I see they can play defense. All of this hot dogging goes out the window at minute one of coach’s first day practice. I agree with him that defense wins games, and it’s the hardest part of the game to learn, especially his system. If enough of these new guys are a “quick study,” there’s an outside chance they go to The Big Dance this year.”

The Big Dance is the NCAA basketball tournament, or “March Madness.” The sloganeers and advertisers can’t get enough of this event. The National Collegiate Athletic Association tourney takes place every year from March into April, and totally dominates all manner of communications, including ill- and legal gambling. When it behooves the U.S. President to offer his predictions as to the outcome, it’s a big deal. Billions of dollars are generated.

I don’t want to get started on the NCAA now, but I will later.

“That’s my best case scenario for this year also,” Cal added, “but it is hard to say. There’s tremendous pressure on these kids. They have to adjust to academics, regardless of how much tutoring they have access to. Sunnyside is not an easy school for anyone. Balancing that with all the practices and travel time, it’s gotta be exhausting. Sure they all get free rides with scholarships, but if you account for all the work they have to put in, it must come to about five cents an hour.”

“Let me ask you something else,” I said. “How do you think these guys stack up against the 1971 team?”

“Well,” Cal said, “My jury is still out on that one. The potential is there, maybe, but guy for guy, I’d have to give the 1971 team the edge. Besides probably having more talent, the leadership on that team was very strong. Slick Sampson and Charlie Bennett were seniors that year, and they led the way. Most of the regular season games were blowouts, but in the close games, you could see they just took over. When the underclassmen looked dazed about the prospect of losing, Sampson and Bennett were in their ears right away. Particularly Charlie; he was a man among a bunch of kids out there on the court."

This comment struck me, because it was the same way I used to describe Charlie.

"I remember that team," Cal continued, "Like they played yesterday."

That remark gave me a shiver, but not enough to swerve the car. "You took the words right out of my mouth," I said. "That's exactly the way I would describe CB."

"This current team though," he continued, "has almost the talent level, but it's all going to come down to experience and leadership. It always does make the difference."

As we're talking, I'm tooling north on Route 20, fortunately on a cool summer night, at 70mph. I chose the radio station this time, the 'Blend' on Sirius. Bingo, Streisand is singing "Happy Days are Here Again."

We both smiled at the appropriateness of the selection.

"I have to start packing when I get home. Phyllis has been packed for a week, and has been bugging me all that time to get started. It's always been her planning versus my last minute. This vacation is for her, as a thank you for putting up with me."

I thought again about my remark about the Bermuda Triangle, and hoped it wasn't going to ruin his trip. "Have a great time, and don't worry about anything." I quickly added, "I'll attend the games with double the enthusiasm, in your absence." I hoped that covered my use of the word 'worry'. We shot the breeze for a few more minutes, until I pulled into his driveway.

Only as I pulled away did I start to think again about the Back Court, the coach, and the link to the Champ team. I was convincing myself that I was in the middle of this as a mediator. I had to somehow get the coach to recognize the achievement of that team, and that it was part of moving forward as a program. However, I was still puzzled why I was the link; why was this now MY calling? Aside from being a diehard fan, what else did I do that made me the chosen one for this?

These thoughts so distracted me, I almost crashed the back entrance gate to the community. I screeched to a halt less than two inches from the gate arm, pressed the remote opener on my dash visor, which allowed me to proceed onto the off road weave through the development that each resident must endure. Since the builder won't put the final grade of macadam on the streets until all the houses are built, all we can do for probably the next three years is to navigate around raised manhole covers, potholes, and parked cars.

I could tell by the number of lights on at the house that Genna was still up, and that I pay the electric bill, not her.

So far tonight, I didn't have any other voices instructing me. Just as I turned off the key and remotely closed the garage door,

"Harry and Byron have something to tell you tomorrow."

I was very pleased that this message came after I stopped driving, and that Someone was listening to me.

* * *

"How did they do?" was Genna's first question as I walked in the door.

"They're looking better each game. It should be a really fun season," I told her. " Cal and Phyllis would love to go to a game, but they're going to Bermuda, so it would have to be the week after next." I could see Genna was only half listening to me; staring intently at the Home and Garden network and fantasizing about a vacation dream home elsewhere in the world. I've joined in watching with her occasionally; a nice respite from the hourly regurgitation of the bad news around the world. This show was about a rental villa in Tuscany, Italy. Ever since I read *Under the Tuscan Sun* by Francis Mayes, and saw the movie I don't know how many times, I've been tempted to resettle there, where my Italian Nana was born. We visited there a few years ago, and I didn't want to leave.

"Let's sell everything and move to Florence!" Genna burst out. "Did you say something about Cal and his wife?"

I chuckled at her suggestion, knowing in the back of my mind, we may someday get serious about the concept.

"Yes, we'll get together the week after next."

"I forgot to look in the mailbox before I left for the game. You didn't take it in, did you?"

Her sheepish nod no was what I expected. "I'll be right back."

On my way to the mailbox in front of the house, I started to think about another way to spring myself, again, to get over to the Ark. Bingo, I think I found it.

The mail bundle was a little on the light side; this being very good, meaning less bills. Once back in the house, I saw a piece of mail from the fund raising arm of Sunnyside. I give what I can from time to time, and also have made a provision in my will. Suffice it to say, I'll never get my name attached to a building, stadium, or arena on campus; not that I'd want to. The letter concluded that I should soon expect a call from the signee, of course.

It's too bad everything is so money driven; like when you get a thank you letter for giving, and on the bottom there's a tear off portion of the letter asking for more.

"Genna, what are your plans tomorrow?" I asked without looking at the calendar.

"Donna next door and I are going to have lunch. She's taking the day off. I think she just wants to vent, that job of hers is stressing her. Then we'll probably window shop, what about you?"

"'Window' is the operative word, correct? Ken Blarney told me at the game earlier that some of the players on the team that can't play in the summer league are playing pickup games at the SAC. He said I could probably sneak in and nobody would bother me. Just for a couple of hours, then I'll have lunch and throw a pint down at Raffael's."

"Sounds like fun."

I really did feel bad about fibbing again and getting away with it. The Sunnyside Athletic Center is the venue that replaced the Ark for sporting events a couple of years after the 1971 team made history there. The fib was that there was a small chance I could get in to watch, but not likely. Thanks to 9/11, I would most likely need a campus ID, and a reason for being there. Much more security was at the SAC than the Ark, it seemed. I would only be there for a few minutes anyway, before high tailing it over to the Ark.

"You always have a good time with Donna. Are you going to turn in soon?"

"Yeah, but first I want to finish cleaning up the kitchen."

I can't understand that about Genna. She turns kitchen cleanup into torture, doing it in installments.

Just get it over with.

"I'm going to wash and brush now, and turn in. If I doze off, and you need something, wake me up," I said with a smirk. The eye roll and sideward glance meant 'not tonight'.

I lay on my back gathering some thoughts. That twilight feeling returned again. Maybe it hasn't left. I realize it during quiet time, or when I'm around the Ark. I remember once when I had a low grade temperature, I felt like this; my senses dulled, with a mild floating sensation. My heavy eyelids were fighting my thoughts about Harry and Bryon, how they figured in my involvement in all this, the coach's attitude, the Back Court ...

Suddenly, one thought smacked my head and almost made me sit up. The only time I had met Harry and Byron, they were together at halftime during a game at the SAC. They were coming down the steps onto the court seating area as I was going up, to the men's room where they probably just were.

"Harry and By, you and the rest of that team saved my life!" I said.

They looked at each other and then me most quizzically, but stopped to hear me out.

"I was out of work at the time. I was really depressed, just hanging around the house feeling sorry for myself, and occasionally thinking worse thoughts than that. I was snapping at my wife; I was really in a bad place. I thought it was all over for me. I did watch a lot of TV, and once while flipping channels, I caught one of the earlier games. The exhilaration of the way you guys played lifted my spirits. I not only was able to get back on track, but I thought of an idea which I eventually turned into a successful business. Just a flip of the TV channel turned my life around, and you guys were in the picture."

"I can't tell you how great it is for us to hear from fans like you. We're gratified that we had that kind of impact on you, and it's great to know that we're still remembered," Harry said, with Byron nodding assent.

That story happened about ten years ago. I was at a game honoring their accomplishment.

They're not remembered as much today, I thought.

It was making more sense to me why I got the call.

Harry and Byron

You know my early morning routine, so we can dispense with that.

I finished with some odds and ends, and I was ready to leave the house around 10 A.M. Genna, my favorite not-a-morning person, was just getting herself in gear. I had already had some cold cereal, and she elected to have the same, a breakfast choice she prefers to concoct on her own. You know. She'll want berries one morning, a banana another. I can never guess her preference on a given morning. So, when she wants cold cereal, at most I just put the bowl and boxes in front of her.

"I'm glad you didn't wake me last night, I was really tired."

She just gave me another one of those John the joker under eyed looks, and grabbed her two percent milk out of the fridge.

"Have fun with Donna," I yelled from the bedroom as I reloaded my pockets with keys, IDs, and a wallet needed to navigate the world outside the house.

Tooling north again on Route 20, I was kind of hoping to get into the SAC. It, too, was beginning to show its age, and it didn't have the charm of the old Ark. It was in need of a serious upgrade, and the fund raising letter I received stated the intention "... to raise five hundred million ... to support students, faculty, programs, and facilities." We basketball fanatics hoped one of those facilities was the SAC.

I pulled into the closest parking lot to the building, got the best space I'll never get during the season, and sauntered over to find an unlocked door in another building.

The side entrance reserved for the media was open, which I found ironic, because I didn't expect there was anything to report or scoop at this time of year.

I walked around the side hallway to the section I usually enter, opened the door to the courtside, and was stunned by the silence that greeted me. Not a sound, just eight thousand empty seats. Not a bouncing ball or a sneaker squeak, just a faint sound of air circulating. Then I realized the guys must have summer classes; they either practiced earlier in the morning, or will later in the day. I glanced down at my season ticket seats, two just off the aisle, several rows up, on a perfect line for a three pointer from the corner. I began wishing it were November already.

"Can I help you?" an official looking middle aged man asked me.

“I was just in the area, and thought I might catch a pickup game.”

“Authorized personnel only,” he said emphatically. “I have to show you the door.”

I had to chuckle as we proceeded towards the front entrance, which was for now a one way out. My first trip to the Ark, I met a ghost, and evaded a watchman; at the SAC, there was no ghost, but I did meet the watchman. Well, I wanted to get over to the Ark anyway.

“You should lock the media entrance; it would make your job even easier,” I offered.

He just scowled, and shuffled back into the tomb he was guarding.

I made a mental note to tell Ken about access to the SAC, but maybe he just had more pull than I.

In twenty minutes, I was over at the Ark. I was wondering if there was another assembly like the other day, to give me another headache watching two time frames. There were many more cars in the lot, so I expected something was going on.

There was no assembly, but I did hear woops and activity at the swimming pool located below decks. It sounded like a swimming meet for adolescents because I could hear a mixture of shrieks from youngsters and parents alike.

The number of students and staff walking around on the court was about the same as the other day; they were oblivious to the Sunny - Mega basketball game playing in their midst. It looked like I was going to get that headache after all.

The game was still in the first half, and the “invisible” scoreboard had Mega up by two. I was on the far side line when I was spotted by Byron Barrett; he motioned for me to cross over the court. I lowered my head; half closed my eyes, and strode towards him with six or seven ghosts passing through on either side of me. Each time, it felt like a whoosh and a slight chill of cooler air swirling around me. I could also hear CB,

Slick, and Q laughing at me. I was also reminded of that twilight feeling again. Just as I got over to the other side line, Byron enters the game for Slick. The coach is talking to Slick, but I can't hear or lip-read what he is saying to him. They both nod agreement about what they discussed, and Slick comes over to me, sweating like an ice cube on a sunny day.

"Slick, how are you and the guys doing?"

"A little bit better at best, John."

It sure didn't sound that way to me, but I let it pass. A little bit worse was more like it. I scanned the gym floor for "real" people who might be staring at me; I felt so out of place, and I was. The foot traffic was minimal, and off to the other side of the floor. Nevertheless, I turned my back to them and whispered.

"Slick, you told me you could remember certain things that have happened to you since this time, but not so much the other way around. Most of this that's going on here is buried in your subconscious in 2011, correct? Did Harry and Byron mention meeting me about ten years ago at the SAC? It may be a key point as to why I'm here."

"They didn't say anything about that; they can't. We can only see certain things about our future that relate to our playing basketball. I know in 2011, as I said, I can still shoot the ball. I don't know anything about a wife, kids, or girlfriends, and it's probably just as well. I just know deep down that something's not right in our future, and we're tormented to keep this replay going without our spirits getting a rest. The other thing I know is you're here to fix it, or try to. I'll take your word that we've met in the future, but remember, when you first showed up at the barn, I didn't know you. We're all taking a leap of faith here. You know a lot more about us than we know about you. You know what's happened to us in the future; and we hope you can change the course of events so that we can rest in peace."

I wanted very badly to tell Slick about his future, especially that he had a beautiful daughter that got all of his basketball genes, and then some. I resisted, feeling an invisible hand over my mouth and an inability to utter a word on the subject. A certain force was reminding me to stick to my mission here: find what I can change about the future that will repair this blip in time.

I realized it didn't matter if Harry and Byron didn't remember meeting me. I was quite certain if they didn't save my life, they certainly changed it for the better. I was sent here to return the favor. The lens was coming into even sharper focus.

This team, without knowing it, was there for me. They are still there for each other. That's the great thing about sports. Once a member on a team so accomplished, it's for life. Graduation, moving away, changing jobs, or starting a family doesn't break the bond. A couple of these guys are hugely successful; they don't need to be here, but they are. Call it loyalty, friendship, or team spirit; it puts them in the same place to muddle through together.

I was starting to feel like a good luck charm, as Sunny rallied to win by eight.

Harry and Byron both smiled at me, and gestured they wanted to shower first before talking. From their sweaty looks and smells, I didn't protest.

Harry had gone on to success like Quincy, but not so much in the basketball profession. He did play a few years in the pros, but injury cut short that career. After a fashion, he settled around Wilmington, Delaware, and did very well as a car dealer, opening up five different franchises in that area, then serving time on the Board of Governors of Sunnyside College.

Byron played a few years overseas, before a long career counseling troubled youth in New Castle County. My guess would be that most ne'er do wells became docile with one look at his imposing frame, and a look from his steely eyes. When I met him ten years ago, he seemed very content with himself.

So, I was getting ready to confront two guys that weren't agonizing over their past; what did they have to tell me?

I heard the shower water stop, so I headed over to the "safe" room to wait for Harry and Byron. I found it odd that showers were of short duration. It was almost like it was the thought that counted, or whatever. I saw a faint glow approach the small window in the door which led toward the locker room.

The door panel seemed to melt as they passed through it, and the room was bathed with two glowing figures, who smiled and one said,

"Hi, John, it's good to finally get a chance to talk to you."

"Same here, Harry." We've talked before, the three of us, I thought. I once again stifled such a remark. "Tell me what you both think is going on here."

"I just remember showing up at this place," Harry began. "I don't know what year it was, not too long after real time; we all just showed up at this old place. At first, I thought it was great, seeing the other guys; we're all back in our prime, and we finally got to beat Mega U. I thought this is heaven; did I die? Then boredom started to set in. Even though the outcome was always different, it was the same team, the same guys, but none of us really talked about it. After many years, Slick was the first to question what was going on, just after you showed up."

Byron was quietly nodding his assent for emphasis. He and Johnny Bird seemed the most shy on the team, but then again, they were only freshman.

"What's your take, Byron?" I asked.

"I think we're all here for Charlie. He's the one who seems to have the most on his mind. He's the one who carried us in the day. I don't know what happened to him, but his bags seem a lot heavier than ours. We all owe him."

"I think you're right, but let me add to that. I'm here because I owe all of you. That Champ season impacted my life in such a way that was nothing short of salvation for me. Beyond that, I know of things that are happening in the present, 2011, that have caused this warp in time, and must be righted to make you all whole and at peace. The powers that be at the present have to be confronted so that your efforts have the true meaning they deserve. I know I must seem to be speaking in code to you, but that's all I can say at this time."

"Does John have anything to add; does he want to speak to me?" I asked further.

"He's here for CB also." He's very shy anyway," offered Byron.

I just smiled, remembering how true this was. Getting words out of John's mouth by a reporter was like pulling teeth instead. His confidence took a quantum leap his sophomore year and beyond, however. "Tell him I'm still here, if he needs me, but I'll be spending most of my time in the present; to fix what's happening here."

"By the way, where are the other guys and what do all of you do in between games?"

"On the other side of the locker room there's a lounge with card and pool tables, a record turntable with any 70s music you can imagine. There's a bunch of vending machines, but ghosts don't have to eat, you know. We just hang around there until they tell us the other team is ready to play."

I was wondering, they didn't have to eat, but they sure did have to shower; why is that? Maybe eating wasn't that closely related to basketball? No matter, I concluded, I have enough real things to figure out.

"So, the Megamont team just shows up, ready to play, then after the game, they just leave? Where do they go?"

Harry said, "We don't know where they come from, and don't know where they go, other than somewhere else in the universe. They're always cleaned up and ready to go. It's like they're visiting us at this jail, which we can't leave, but they come and go as they please."

I hear ya, Harry, I thought, but it was slightly painful to think of the Ark as a jail. Maybe it was that first day of orientation, but not during the rest of my time there.

"Tell the other guys I'm on the case, and I'll be working hard for them," as I waved goodbye to the both of them.

A few minutes later, I was at Raffael's in downtown Wilmington. On the way I passed the site where I took Genna on our first date, which is now a grassy knoll. I saddled up to the bar, and ordered a pint of Bass ale before I even hit the seat. I love Raff's hanger steak for dinner, but it was lunchtime, and at my age, a salad with grilled shrimp would leave me feeling better afterwards. I slowly sipped the suds while waiting for the salad, and started to formulate my plan to save the souls that saved mine. However, I realized it had to go beyond them; they were just a symbol of what was wrong with college sports.

"What kind of dressing would you like with the salad, sir?" as the waiter whizzed the dish past my right ear, plopped the plate on the bar, almost cracking it.

"House," I said to him, "and another pint of Bass," to the bartender.

I had plenty of time to distill the two pints before heading back to Marlton.

Chapter Six

It was not going to be easy for me to get Coach Manny Wheaton to see things my way. He was in his late 30s, and probably involved in the game before he could remember. As I think I alluded to before, he's a coach's son; so instead of a pacifier, he most likely had a lemon sized softball to suck on. Actually, it may have been a lemon because he was tough as nails. He had success all along the way from Biddy to Division I college ball, playing point guard for a successful program. He had an inside track to pick his father's brain about the game. I don't know for sure, but I don't think Manny's father pushed him as much as Manny pushed himself. My guess is coach had a passion, love, and drive for the game; more than his father's genes or knowledge of the game.

Before coming to Sunnyside, he paid his dues assisting a few of the better coaches in the Northeast, all of whom enhanced the fundamentals of his game to ensure success when Manny went off on his own. The coaching fraternity is like any other area of business; it's about relationships, and Manny sure forged alliances with high school coaches, and all the other movers and shakers around the sport.

Manny Wheaton cut his teeth as a head coach at a small school in the Philly area, and after a few successful years of getting one hundred and ten per cent out of everyone from his staff down to the water boy, he was ready for Sunnyside and the Coastal East, the best basketball league in the country.

Just one year at Sunny was all it took for everyone to take notice. It wasn't that the won-lost record improved, but he changed the spirit and the culture around the sport. He had a way of getting everyone involved, not just players, to run through brick walls for him. That was all he had to do to convince the local high school coaches that Manny Wheaton was to be trusted with the very good, and then great players, they would be sending him in years to come.

This was the person, who knew nothing but success on the hardwood, whose philosophy of his, or the highway, who I had to convince was wrong about something relating to basketball.

"Check, please," I yelled to the waiter. After settling with him, I strode toward the men's room. The two Bass pints had just about run their course.

I decided the next step was an email to Ken Blarney, the Back Court president, regarding the 1971 team being honored by the AD. I had to expand on this idea to go further than that. I was looking to change the whole culture regarding all former players at Sunnyside. This tough sell was going to get tougher.

I was in the Eos weaving south on Route 20 again, wondering how Genna's day went with Donna, and which couple of fibs would be suitable regarding the pickup game at the SAC.

* * *

I got back to the house in Marlton before Genna returned from her excursion with Donna. The best half-fib I could come up with was that there was no scrimmage at the SAC (true), so I went down to Raffael's and had one too many pints (half true); so I sat around at the bar until the pints had run their course (half true). I was hoping she wouldn't even ask, because I wouldn't have to say anything.

In the meantime, I went to our loft office to think about what to say to Ken Blarney in an email about the coach.

Bingo, I had an idea. I remembered the question I asked the coach at a Back Court meeting last fall: if he had any plans to reach out to former players, to bring their interest back into the program. A few years, and a couple of coaches ago, there was strong involvement in this area. Everyone, I think, benefitted; the fans and players, who are always prone to reunions and reminiscing, as well as the program, which had many extra pairs of eyes that could spot talent. I rethought the answer Manny Wheaton gave me. At the time, I thought it was an area that he didn't want to get involved in, at least at that point. Now I thought that just might not be the case. He may, I thought, want to see it done, but now he doesn't really have the time. After all, the immediate need was to get the right players, teach them his system, and come up with a winner. The first couple of years, this is a 24/7 job for sure.

What if I could convince Ken, then the two of us convince coach that the Back Court could do this for him? The more I thought about it, the more I thought he would go along with it. He blew Ken off about recognizing the 1971 team due to the time constraints I just mentioned. I could do this, but I would have to go in through the back door.

I smiled to myself at the thought of "back door," because it was a perfect analogy in basketball parlance. The "back door" is a play where the motion offense draws the defense away from the basket with their eyes focused toward one side of the court, while an offensive player slipping behind them streaks to the basket to receive a pass for an easy layup. When executed properly, it's a thing of beauty, with a high percentage of success; just the outcome I am hoping for.

"Ken," I started the email. "I think the Back Court should propose taking on the responsibility of getting former players reacquainted with the program by inviting them to our meetings during the upcoming season. Doing this, I think, would also be a boost to club membership as well. The way to go about this is to float the idea past the Athletic Director, Larry Dariani. I've met him a couple of times, and he's always graciously answered my emails about my past concerns for the program. If you like, I'll draft a concept letter to him to gauge his reaction. Let me know if you want to proceed with this. I'll ghost write it with your name as President of the BC."

Every time I think or say the word ghost lately, I still shudder a bit. As you may have guessed, I'm proposing this idea with the 1971 team in mind; they're the ones I ultimately want to see benefit.

Ken usually gets back to me quickly, smart phone in hand. I don't have one, so I would check the computer later.

In the loft, I can hear the garage door open, which it just did, telling me Genna was home. I trotted downstairs, just in time to hear her entering the mud room with what sounded like a rustling of packages.

Before I could open my mouth, she said, "I got a pair of shoes on sale, sandals for the rest of the summer, and wait until you see what I got us for supper!"

Pure Genna, I chuckled to myself. When she gets something for herself, she usually gets me a little something. She knows, and I know what she's doing, but neither cares.

"Broiled tilapia, stuffed with shrimp and scallops, in a mild diablo sauce!" she said while she slurped, raised her eyebrows twice, and smiled.

"Sounds good to me. Only one pair of shoes, "such a deal!" for me, I thought.

"Do you want to eat now, or wait?" she asked.

"I can wait. I want to check my email. I'm expecting a note from Ken."

Sure enough, I opened my mail folder, and there's Ken.

"John, I think it's an excellent idea, bouncing it off Larry D. first. If he likes it, I'm sure he'll put pressure on the men's program, and be on our side." Ken.

I had taken the liberty of drafting a letter beforehand, so I said this,

"Ken, here's the draft. This is what I had in mind,"

"The Back Court is transforming into a more ambitious organization that will not only raise valuable funds for the basketball program, but will also serve as a resource for former players who may be looking to network with Sunnyside supporters. We are working very hard to put

Coach Manny Wheaton in a position where he can look a recruit and his family in the eye, and tell them Sunny will be there for them for the rest of their life.

We truly hope that you will consider our offer and become involved. If you aren't able to make it back to campus often, please drop us a line, fill us in on what you're doing, and offer suggestions on how we can make the Back Court as effective as possible."

"If this is OK with you, I'll let it fly." John.

"Go for it!" Ken said moments later.

I wouldn't be hearing from the AD, Larry Dariani, for at least several days; he has more balls to juggle that a lottery drawing.

My stomach led me back downstairs to the stuffed tilapia in the kitchen. It sounded tasty, but, a strange combo for a dish. Tilapia was considered the fish that Jesus used in the miracle of the loaves and fishes. 'Diablo' meant "of the devil." Regardless, I couldn't wait to try it.

"How about I sauté an onion and some green beans; they'll go good with that sauce on the fish?" I asked her.

"Knock yourself out."

I can never quite figure out if Genna likes my cooking suggestions more than the fact I'm doing it.

We weren't disappointed by the meal. Good and evil can go well together, I thought.

"How was Raffael's?"

Not, "how was the scrimmage at the SAC," nor an accounting of my time spent.

"Very good, as usual," I said. "What's on tap for tonight?"

"I want to catch up on some news, and then I guess I'll read awhile."

I rolled my eyes when she said news.

"If I watch the news over the next few days, I'm afraid I may kill myself." The country was going through a viciously mean spirited and uncivil "debate," if I can call it that, which had me wishing that all our elected officials be recalled, and new replacements sent to try their hand at governing. As I was thinking this way, I realized I needed a break from politics.

"Ken and I are working on a few new things for the Back Court, and I want to give them some thought."

I went upstairs to the office, and started to wish and hope I was on the right track; that my charges at the Ark would find peace through me. Once again I was reminded of that queasy, twilight numbness which for days has crept into my quiet time.

"Thanks in advance."

This time, it was just a whisper, but it spoke volumes to me that my course was true.

* * *

"John, are you alright? I haven't heard a peep out of you in three hours. It's bedtime. I'm going to bed, but not to sleep."

Hearing that, I was now wide awake. I thought of my mother-in-law's comment, back in the day when Genna and I thought we were both rabbits:

"That kid has SOME shape!" Rest her soul, was she right. After forty-two years, I can tell you, she's still got it; and I don't have cataracts. We have gradually shifted from quantity to quality over the years, but I'm not trying to influence your sex lives. I'll see you all in the morning.

* * *

Good morning. Wow.

The morning walk was very brisk, around 7 A.M. before another hazy, humid day began forming. I thought of the Lerner and Loewe song from "My Fair Lady,"

"I have often walked down this street before. But the pavement always stayed beneath my feet before …"

Some days, the walk is not a chore. I was nearing the house when a chilly gust of wind swirled past me, much like a frontal change in the weather. I was getting conditioned to this occurrence.

"You have mail from Larry."

Another message, delivered as gently as the last one. I jogged the rest of the way to the house, entered as quietly and quickly as possible, so as not to awaken Sleeping Beauty. I sidestepped as many creaking floor boards as possible up to the loft office, and logged into my mail. It surprised the hell out of me to hear from him so fast, Somebody must be pulling strings for me.

"Hi, John, it's always good to hear from you. I think the idea is terrific, but I want you to contact the basketball office to run it by them."

I was a little anxious about his response. Although he indicated support, he may be leaving it up to the coach to decide to go forward or not with it. Or maybe, he wanted to honor the chain of command; no back door plays by him.

Regardless, I forwarded his response to Ken, who was jubilant.

"This is a great start! I'm supposed to have a sit down with Coach Wheaton in the near future. I'm going to send your letter to the basketball office, which will give me something else to talk to him about. Maybe I can request that you tag along, since this new mission of the BC is largely your idea. What do you say?" Ken.

"I'm game. It'll be great to see firsthand how he beats people up, lol! I'm flexible, time wise, as you know. Just give me a few days notice." John.

This is turning out to be a great day already, I thought. I heard the master bathroom door close, signaling Genna was up. I went downstairs to meet her in the kitchen.

"This establishment comes with free breakfast the next morning," I said a few moments later as she sat in her usual place.

"I know, and you can wipe that smirk off your face now. Didn't you get some bagels from Wagner's the other day? I'll have a half with cream cheese, and a slab of wild caught salmon on top. I'll make my own coffee."

Easy enough, as I toasted her bagel. When she says "bagel," she means toasted. I opted for a blueberry Greek yogurt, half a banana, and orange juice with a tablespoon of flaxseed mixed in. I passed the other half of the banana over to her.

"Do you want to hike over to Long Beach, if you have no plans for today?" I asked.

"Sure, and after I do as much window shopping as I want, you can take me for a late lunch at Sirenelli's on the boardwalk." This time, she had the smirk. I was glad she said lunch, instead of supper, which would entail much more shopping; but then again, Genna knows just how far she can push me.

"You drive a hard bargain."

"You know I don't come cheap."

Did I ever.

Chapter Seven

Long Beach is another one of those Delaware shore towns that have enjoyed resurgence during recent years, and the blighted areas were gradually being turned over. The second thing that comes to mind is Long Beach reminds me of Long Branch, New Jersey, having spent a good deal of my childhood around that area, where Bruce Springsteen gave birth to "Born to Run" in about three weeks time, so I've heard. I wonder if any cosmic voices helped him lay that one down. Another work of genius for what it is, composed in a very short time.

Route 20 is like the aorta for us and these shore towns like Long Beach, Baybury Park, and Bella Vista, all feeding off it like lungs and hearts. The temperature had risen to about our threshold for an Eos top down; but we had it down anyway, breezing toward the shore where it would be cooler.

Let's skip the shopping part. I hate to do it; I hate to even think about it. Yet sometimes, I do it for love.

We sat outside on the deck at Sirenelli's. By that time, the sun had passed over towards the west, and we were in the shade, with a cool sea breeze off the ocean. The surf and breeze are reminders to me to come back, from whence I came, to the sea.

The waitress was kind enough to start the happy hour clock a little early for us. So after a couple of Genna's Cosmos, and my Gin and Tonics, we were ready to tackle their crab cake special. We usually order different items, then share, but not when we order crab cakes. These were good, a close second to those at the Crab Trap in Somers Point, around Atlantic City, NJ.

Soon enough, we were back in the car heading to Marlton. As you probably guessed, Genna was snoozing next to me, her sleep-in-car syndrome in full effect, enhanced by the open air foiling around the Eos.

I was feeling extra lucky today, hoping Ken had already heard back from the coach's office. If I got such a quick response from Larry Dariani; it could happen again, like lightning. I would know soon enough.

"Genna, we're home."

"I just loooove to ride in that car with the top down."

"Me, too," I said, "and I got you home in time for the bad news shows. I think we can skip dinner, and just have a snack later, no? I'll be up at the computer."

"OK. I'll call you if I hear my stomach rumble."

"You've got mail" from Ken appeared on the screen.

"John, things are happening pretty quickly. I did get a reply from Coach Wheaton, but it was very curt and noncommittal whether he likes the idea or not. He wants to meet the both of us as soon as possible, and he mentioned he has an hour tomorrow afternoon at 3 P.M. at the Ark on Colters Ave. That's shorter notice than you like, but does it still work for you? Don't ask me why we're meeting at the Ark, instead of his office in the SAC. Anyway, that's the deal. We'd better be prepared. Are you game?" Ken.

"I'll be waiting for you on the basketball court, at 3 P.M. I'll be prepared to tell him that our idea is going to make it easier for him to sell the program." John.

The Ark! Why does he want to meet us at the Ark? Maybe he has a function on the main campus, which is wrapped around 3 P.M. and he doesn't want to hike back and forth. That possibility is less worrisome than his curt response to Ken. He may not have appreciated my "back door" play with the AD, feeling I should have come to him first. I guess I'll be ready to apologize profusely, and play dumb, claiming protocol was never my strong suit. On the other hand, he certainly isn't that thin-skinned. Maybe I am wrong, and he doesn't feel this is the right time to make a push in this direction. Maybe he feels that since everyone loves a winner, these alums will return when a better won-lost record does. Well, I'll find out tomorrow at three. With the worst case scenario, I'll just plant the seed for a future endeavor.

Aside from this, there's my problem with my ghostly friends at the Ark. It's going to be a neat trick for me to concentrate, dealing with a very intense individual in Coach Wheaton as well as Slick and the gang if they decide to clown around. Then again, they may be very serious, realizing I'm doing this for them.

I decided to take a break from this topic, and join Genna to watch how much further the world fell apart since yesterday.

Same old, same old. I never realized before we elected a Black President, how far from over the Civil War was. I was able to withstand about a half hour of bigotry and racism, under the guise of debate and patriotism, before I had to run into the other room, and picked up the book I was reading, ironically for me, titled *Your Voice in My Head* by Emma Forrest. It's an autobiographical story about a troubled young woman who was being greatly helped by a psychiatrist, who tragically dies while she is still in treatment. She is able to keep herself together by asking herself what the doctor would say if he were still here. She finds salvation, and retells it in utterly beautiful prose, making a dreary subject inspiring.

I have voices in my head, also, and a promise to keep, and miles to go before I sleep. Thank you, Robert Frost.

* * *

I arrived at the Ark parking lot about 2:45. A company I used to work for had, as part of its corporate culture, a policy of all its executives setting their watches fifteen minutes ahead of real time. I no longer did this, but I still seem to arrive around fifteen minutes early anyway. I'm sure anxiety contributed to my arrival time. The more I thought about this meeting last evening and through fitful sleeplessness, the more of a sense I had that the meeting was going to go badly. After my morning usual, I spent the rest of it gardening. I tend to do that when I'm trying to work through something mentally. To me, gardening and thinking go together. When I was finished outside, there wasn't a weed or bug bitten leaf to be found.

I parked the Eos, and headed for my usual door. The fact that I was going through the 'back door' of the Ark didn't even give me a chuckle.

After walking into the Ark, I saw Ken Blarney standing at center court, looking as anxious as I was. My other friends were nowhere to be seen, by me of course. I was hoping they would take the day off because my level of concentration was and is never that good.

"Coach asked us to meet him in that little supply room at the far end of the court. It's little used, and no one should bother us there. John, are you alright?"

Ken must have noticed the blood drain from my face when he said "supply room."

"I'm OK, just not much sleep last night. I would have thought there was an office he could use here."

"There are offices, but they must all be in use today. I'm sure that didn't put him in a good mood. As you saw on the court last year, he doesn't take kindly to little things that go wrong," Ken added. "Let's get this over with."

As we walked toward the supply room, I let Ken walk slightly ahead, so I could glance around the rest of the Ark to see if I was being watched, so to speak.

Ken opened the door, and we noticed that Coach Wheaton was just barely inside, so that when we walked in, he was in our faces, without a hello or a handshake.

"Ken, the Back Court sucks, so you must suck. You guys have no money. You sell a few 50/50 raffle tickets, which is enough for your little group to sit around and stuff your face with pizza, while me or a member of my staff has to regale you with inside dope about the program. You're going to have to come up with a better plan than that to justify your existence. And John, don't you EVER, don't you F* * ***G ever go over my head with a basketball matter again."

Manny Wheaton's eyes were like brown lasers that kept scanning between Ken's and my peeps, trying to gauge a reaction. His face was purple, and I expected a drop of blood to trickle from his ear that instant.

We were being talked to like members of his team. A glance by me at Ken noticed an emotion between fear and anger. I would have said just anger, but I could see him tremble slightly.

This demeanor by coach was what I had a gut feeling about, which caused a half day's worth of anxiety. However, now that he put his first card on the table, I was ready to play my hand, also. Despite this outburst, I was surprised he remembered my name from the Back Court meeting. I gathered he wasn't big on small talk, and since he knew the both of us, dispensing with introductions and handshakes was predictable.

Given these calculations, and noticing that Ken was still a little shell shocked, I decided to respond first.

By nature, I'm a calm person; so I wasn't going to respond in kind. However, I wasn't going to take that kind of talk from someone young enough to be my son.

"Coach, Ken doesn't suck, and I don't suck. Since I'm not on scholarship here, you don't have a right to talk to me that way, so don't do it again. We're all on the same team here, and we realize the past was not as productive as it should have been, both on and off the court. We want to move forward. We know how hard you're working, and we want to compliment your efforts. We both want to put more fannies in the seats. Don't take it as a slight that I contacted Larry Dariani before you. Now that I know you better, all future ideas will go through your office first."

I noticed that his cheeks were more of a pinkish tone, and I was no longer looking for blood in his ear.

"We're trying to think long term here. Look, the AD's office is swamped, as is yours. These budget cutbacks have been brutal to the work force at the school. Larry's very media savvy; that's his background. The program's getting much better exposure. You're a coach who can recruit, coach a good game, and get the most effort on the court. What we in the club want to do is take care of the future of these kids. Most of them see the big letters NBA just ahead of them, and it doesn't pan out that way for most. The National Basketball Association is only for a select few. We want to cushion the basketball afterlife of these kids. They shouldn't be thought of as a box of Kleenex that lasts three or four years and then is empty. If we can do this, it sets us apart from most other schools, and it can be a great selling tool for you. This philosophy will help keep the program at the high level you are about to attain. What's your shoe size, coach?" I asked him quickly, which seemed to catch him off guard.

"Eleven."

"There are a couple of Hall of Fame coaches in the Coastal East that are both size twenty. They'll both be retiring soon enough. Rather that you trying to fit your size 11 into their size 20, we want your feet to stay and grow at Sunnyside. We don't want you to go to one of those schools to trip and fall."

Ken finally chimed in, "Coach, if we find ways to bring the basketball alums back to the program, there's a revenue stream increase. We'll handle it. All we need is for the basketball office to mail our communications out, to respect the alum's privacy. Gradually, they'll come back."

Coach Wheaton was pondering as we were talking, but he was tough to read. After a short while, he said, "Let me sleep on this. I'll give you an answer in the morning."

He shook both our hands, which he didn't do as a greeting, and was out the door. Ken and I stared at each other before Ken said,

"What's your take?"

"Well," I said, "He must like the singer, Meatloaf."

Ken smirked and said, "I think he's going to go for it. He had to spank us for your back door play, but at the end of the day, I think he liked what you had to say."

"Based on the way the conversation was going, I didn't see an opportune time to ask him about the 1971 team," I said.

"Probably just as well, gauging by his mood; and I believe he is still adamant not wanting to draw a comparison between his teams at Sunnyside, and them." Ken had that "don't shoot the messenger" look on his face again.

"That's just plain silly. What's he afraid of? He's said that he wants to win a championship, and doing that means winning the Final, not coming up short. Why doesn't he see their performance as a goal to surpass? Ken, I still feel we have to pursue this. I'd like to get him and Larry Dariani in the same room to talk about this; we'd probably stand a better chance. Larry is a Sunny Grad, and our tradition means more to him than Manny."

"I think you're right, John. If you really want to pursue it, that would be the way to go about it."

We walked out of that supply room, and I saw my six clean uniformed friends somberly staring at me. Behind them, the Mega U. team was warming up.

"Ken, I'm going to hit the head before I leave. I hope to speak to you in the morning, as the coach suggested." I hoped he didn't have to use the facilities, so I could spend some more time with my favorite Caspers.

"I'll call you as soon as I hear from coach." He departed the building through the back door.

* * *

"What?" I asked.

I had forgotten myself, and where I was, and several onlookers turned around to see me talking to myself. I quickly recovered and walked over towards the supply room, and the team followed me. I also realized how "normal" I now felt around these ghosts. The Mega players continued to warm up, not missing a beat.

Once in the room with the door closed, I said, "Why the long faces? I'm just getting started with this guy. I guess you heard what the new coach had to say. He's a tough customer, but I'm going to work on him. I've got a long row to hoe here, so don't you guys get down on me so soon. One way or another, I'll get him to come around. In the meantime, I know all about your salvation, because it's mine, too. Try to have a little more fun, you're all still in your prime, remember."

From the looks on their faces, they saw this pitch to be a curveball in the dirt, and none of them was swinging at it.

Charlie Bennett spoke as his hound dog eyes peered at me, "John, none of us liked the way he treated you and that other guy with you. Our coach treats everyone with respect. Sure he's hard on us, but we know he respects us, and vice versa. He would never speak to a fan or a booster like this guy did. He just can't blow off everyone like that."

I knew exactly what CB was talking about. The previous coach had been fired, but not before he threw hand grenades at the program, the Back Court, and everyone and thing connected to it.

"I hear you," I replied, "the 'other guy' is Ken Blarney, the current President of the Back Court. He's going to help me help you, without really knowing it. Look, what you guys wanted to happen in 1971 is going to happen with this coach; I'm certain of it. I can see why you think he's going about it the wrong way, but that will change. The coach has a strong AD he works for, someone who went to Sunnyside, who knows what you guys were all about. This coach is not like a suit you buy off the rack. He's custom made. He needs a little letting out here; taking in a little there… You know what I mean?"

My sincerity must have shown, because this fastball over the plate was a hit to them. Grins and smiles took over their faces which made me happy.

At that very moment, it started.

I heard a very slight rumbling, as if from a bull dozer working on a construction site one block away. The rumbling turned to a mild vibration like I felt from my electric shaver in the morning which then overtook my entire body, and I started to shake.

I wasn't the only one. The spirits in the room, all of whom were happy a few moments ago, were exchanging dart-like glances at each other and me. Being the only one in the room whose feet were anchored to the ground, I found it difficult to remain standing. The shelves in the room were swaying, and their contents began tumbling to the floor. I wobbled over to the door, recalling a grade school safety suggestion that a door jamb was a structurally safe place to be during a tremor. I ripped open the door, sat down, and braced my feet on one side of the opening, while feeling the hinge dig into my back on the other. My gaze kept glancing onto the open court, then into the supply room. The Mega players were showing as much concern as their opponents, but the 2011 denizens were starting to panic. Struggling to their feet after falling, they were screaming, walking, and crawling towards the exits. I saw the Ark's old walls starting to crack, window panes seeming to explode, and dirt, dust, as well as paints chip cascade like a dirty snowstorm onto the court.

I started to think it may be time to meet my Maker when a curdling voice snarled at me.

"These souls in here are MINE!!! I own them, and YOU cannot take them from ME! YOU should leave now, before I claim YOU as well."

The words were not delivered with just sound waves, but crackling thunderbolts that seemed to numb and nearly puncture my eardrums.

A few seconds passed, and my muscles started to tense, started to accept this new, fearsome advice that toyed with my emotions, and I tried to gather enough strength to get to the back door.

“No I won’t,”

I thought to myself a split second after that. I’ve prayed for goodness and good advice all my life, and this is BAD. A lifetime of faith in every fiber of me wasn’t going to waste in a small moment in time.

More quickly and abruptly than they started, the tremors stopped. I had closed my eyes after I made the right decision to stay, and a more soothing, familiar voice spoke to me.

“Fear no longer my other, wayward son. He now knows he cannot tempt you. The path you are still on is true. Your belief in me sooths my heart.”

I opened my eyes to discover the impending doom I witnessed was imagined. Yes, there was a minor tremor, enough to awaken the hazy dust now filtering onto the court, but the Ark was otherwise intact. The real people continued to mill around, chuckling and making jokes about living in California. The spirits in the supply room were shrugging, but must have noticed I looked a bit ragged.

“John, are you OK?”

Slick queried me as I regained my footing while expelling some dust from my throat.

“I’m fine now. Never felt better, actually. Say, did any of you hear any voices just a few moments ago?”

As they looked at each other, they all got the “is he sure he’s alright” look on their collective faces.

“No,” Charlie replied. “All we had was a little earthquake that lasted about ten seconds. It’s best the dust and paint chips came down then, rather than in a game like they used to. Are you sure you’re OK?”

“Really, I am. Now where was I? Oh yes, the coach. Believe me, he’s the right guy, and he’s going to bring us a championship. You’ve got to hang in there. It's going to be a small fraction of forty years for me to right this, I promise. Now go kick Mega's ass, again."

The Megamont players continued to warm up as I was talking to Charlie and his teammates. As the Sunny players sauntered onto the court, the Mega team gathered around the half court jump circle. The Megamont team was like a long playing record that just looped around and around; only when the Sunny stylus was in place, did they begin to play.

I was tempted to take advantage of my time warp, and watch those two teams play again, but I decided to leave, to keep ahead of the traffic on Route 20 South. As I left, I felt a new sense of purpose, as a stronger person for the rest of my life.

Chapter Eight

As I hoped, I was just in front of the rush hour traffic on Route 20; the crest of the wave of cars was close behind me. I was listening to Bloomberg radio recount the carnage of the day on Wall Street when the phone cut into the broadcast. It was Calvin.

"Hey, John, are we still on for tonight?"

I paused for a split second before recovering. I had totally forgotten the double date we had made with Cal and his wife Phyllis. We had cancelled once because Genna had a migraine, so I quickly added, "Sure, Cal, what time should we be at your house?"

"Come by about 7 P.M. The playoff game doesn't start until 9, so we can have a pizza at Focaccio's on the same corner where the gym is."

"Sounds good. See you then."

When I arrived home, to rub in my forgetfulness, Genna said, "Aren't we seeing Cal and Phyllis tonight for pizza and a game?"

"Yes. He called on my way home. Is your back up to it?"

Genna has always had chronic back problems, noticed by me shortly after we were married. I called her "the rambling wreck". I kidded her that her alma mater, St. Peters in Jersey City, New Jersey, was actually a satellite school of Georgia Tech (... Rambling wreck from Georgia Tech … the old fight song goes). I also kiddingly chided her father, rest his soul, for not offering full disclosure regarding the goods I was getting.

"I'll be fine. Let's not forget those cushions though."

"We've got about two hours. Do you want a cocktail on the deck?"

"You make the margaritas, and I'll put out the lounge chairs and cushions," Genna replied.

I delved into the freezer for the premixed margaritas, and set the container on the island countertop. I grabbed our two favorite oversized martini glasses with the palm trees etched on the side, limed and salted the rims, scooped that heavenly slush until a small mountain was in each. Two small demitasse spoons and napkins completed the drinks. A brain freeze was just around the corner. I got my shades and cap, and waltzed the drinks over to the small table between the lounges.

"Cheers!" we both said, and clinked for good luck.

This time of day, the sun's rays are just piercing the tops of the trees to the west, giving our faces a dappled bath. We were both just absorbing this feeling, and not saying much, meditating with our thoughts from the day.

Twilight, which wasn't upon the area yet, was upon me. The feeling I drifted in and out of since my encounters over the past few days began again. Was it the margarita? I do make a stiff one. I felt a cool breeze, like the ones before the messages were delivered, but not a word was said. Just a reminder, I thought, which really wasn't necessary….

"John, wake up. We have to get going."

I looked over at my empty glass. "I don't even remember finishing my drink."

"You didn't, I did. You looked so peaceful; I didn't want to wake you. Besides, you're driving us to Calvin's."

I looked at her smirk and said, "I guess a kind way to describe you is "luscious." I'll go put on my uniform."

I grabbed a rayon blue shirt that had discreet, small Sunny logos on the front and back, put on jeans and sneakers. Quite a contrast to Genna, as always, who dresses to the nines whenever she's going out the front door. I'm usually the tramp to her lady for these types of events.

"Top down?" I asked. We were only traveling five minutes to Cal's, but I knew her answer.

"Of course!"

Phyllis and Genna were both teachers. They seemed to hit it off, and slid right into that subject. Cal and I started discussing the team's chances for the evening.

"I just read on the team message board that we're going to be without three players, the guys from the DC area. Summer school just got out, so they headed home, deserting their teammates." Cal seemed slightly livid as he said this. Being a former high level player, I could understand his viewpoint.

"I hear you, but these might just be homesick kids, missing mom's cooking. I think they accomplished what they had to. The last few games were pretty good from the standpoint of meshing together, and they did give the first place team their only loss. Are they going to win tonight, or the tourney? No. They should be out of gas after the first half. The pizza place could be the highlight of the evening."

The pizza at Focaccio's was very good. It had a thin, crispy crust. Cal and Phyllis ordered their half jalapeno, and when it was delivered I noticed that none of the seeds of the pepper had been removed. I looked around to find the nearest fire extinguisher for them. Genna and I stuck with our plain cheese half. I like jalapeno peppers chilled without the seeds. Despite complaining about the heat, Cal and Phyllis did manage to finish their half pie without smoke coming out of their ears. I'm sure the quart of water each drank helped.

"Let's go see some good basketball," Cal said excitedly.

"For the first half, anyway," I reminded him.

Ours was the second game of the doubleheader, and the first game was running long. While waiting in the lobby for the game to end and the seats to empty, I spotted Karen Wheaton, the coach's wife. Ken Blarney had pointed her out during a previous game. And I noticed her texting the entire time. The NCAA rules don't allow the coach to be present at these games, but she probably smart phoned him all he needed to know.

Karen seemed like a delightful person by first observation. She was very supportive, and profusely thanked the Sunny fanatics for their efforts in return. I was quite certain coach didn't talk to her like he did to Ken and me.

"Hi, Karen. Are you ready to tickle that QWERTY keyboard?" I asked.

"Yeah. This is a tough time of the year for Manny. For him, he starts thinking up offensive and defensive schemes for these guys. He can be very irritable until he gets things clear in his head. I just step aside and let him go."

"It must be tough having so many new guys," I offered. "Not knowing how their skills will perform at this new level."

I thought this was probably contributing to his short fuse in dealing with us earlier in the day. I chuckled to myself as I thought of him as a coach in heat.

"Karen, coach has a lot of support and confidence that he'll get it done. The Back Court in particular wants to drum up more support on its own to shoulder some of the load for him." I couldn't resist getting a plug in here.

"I know that. He's still getting used to the community and traditions here. I'm sure it will all come together. Thanks again for all your support." She turned away, and greeted a few other fans. A great asset for coach, I thought, and something both he and I have in common; we both married "UP".

I found these comments by her to be very insightful, and couldn't wait to share them with Ken, hoping he was here tonight. I didn't see him in the lobby, so I thought he might be watching the first game.

The first game ended, and the majority of fans left the building. As they thinned out, I could see Ken sitting in the first row courtside.

"Hey, Ken, I just spoke to Karen, the coach's wife, and based on her comments, I agree that he is going to come around to our viewpoint. She said his head is overloaded with new offensive and defensive schemes, trying to figure out which will work best with the new guys. She was very helpful in my understanding of what makes him tick."

"This is good news," Ken added. "Soon as I hear anything …" From the coach, he meant.

We were correct in our pre-game assessment. The team played hard for a little more than a half, before rigor mortis set in. They finished out the game looking like they were already on vacation, too.

On the way home, I steered the conversation away from the game, because I could see Cal was still seething about the three guys that bailed on their teammates. We talked about our sons, and generally the four of us hit it off and agreed to meet again soon. They waved goodbye as we drove from their house.

We were home again, six minutes later. It took one minute to put the top down, and five minutes to roll down the street.

* * *

It was twilight time again; for me, that is. The real sunset occurred back at the pizza parlor hours ago. I was winding down this day, alone with my thoughts while Genna was removing her daily makeup face and starting her regenerative ritual to slow down Father Time's "character lines", as I call them, on her face,. The sun seemed to set on me again as my thoughts drifted back to 1971, and the privileged view back in time it affords me. This night I had a queasy feeling, like being on a boat at the apex of a long arching wave. It's a feeling of weightlessness, but continuous, not fleeting. I was in suspension, just like the 1971 team at the Ark.

I didn't remember falling asleep, but here I was waking up to the sheer filtered sunlight entering the room. Genna was on her silent left side, her body twisted like she was in a car wreck. I still had that floating feeling which I didn't expect to lose until I got up and put some other thoughts in my head. I was expecting to hear from Ken this morning if Coach Wheaton kept his word. Ken had the Back Court going in the right direction. He had a bunch of other creative initiatives besides my idea of the former player push. Coach Wheaton wasn't all wrong characterizing the club as he did. The BC lacked any real impact to enhance the basketball program. The time was right for it to make a push. We had a new AD on the way up who had a great one-two punch for selling donors; a left hook to the heart, and a right cross to the wallet. We had a new coach on the way up who had his own winning combo; a chess master on game day, and a surrogate father to the top recruits who were buying what he was selling. It was the right time for the BC to jump on the surfboard with these guys, and ride the wave we've all been waiting for. It really did seem everything was coming together.

"You've got mail from Ken."

The tone of the voice whisper implied that breakfast would wait. I logged in.

"Coach wants us to have a meeting soon with him and Larry Dariani, hopefully within the week. That's it, that's all he said, no for or against our idea. I'll keep you posted." Ken.

"If his answer was a flat out 'no', the easiest way to deliver it would be email, correct?" I shot back. "We're still alive on this one."

I logged off, and tiptoed down into the kitchen. I poured some orange juice and added some flaxseed; this helps keep my cholesterol around one sixty. It was drizzling outside, and I don't like to use the treadmill in the basement in the summer. I sipped on the OJ, and settled into a family room chair to finger my rosary beads; offering prayers to my usual suspects in need of assistance, and hoping this all comes together. Soon my prayer whispers were silenced by the whisper in my ears.

"John, I alone have given you this task, and you must try to do it on your own. You may fail in your own eyes, but I will be the judge of your efforts. The reason you have been given life, is to make other life better. You were born in a better part of your world, into much love that continues to this day. Your elder family has given you much, you have been good to them in return, and I have blessed you with their longevity. You have been given many other things; not riches, but not the poverty which has enslaved most of your world. I ask you to judge yourself. Have you given nearly what you have received in life? Is the ledger of your life in balance? Nature only needs balance to thrive. Those beings who have taken more return as matter less fortunate, and the opposite is also true."

"What you must do is beyond what you are thinking now. Expand your effort to help many more. Your world may or may not survive what is going on now; too much is being taken, but I will not judge you as I will judge them. Your prayers make me feel like a good Father, I need to keep hearing them."

I noticed that the rosary beads had slipped from my hand. There was silence once again, and I could sense a wavy aura around me and the recliner I lay on. The wavy light was akin to a mirage in the desert. I thought I was in a desert, lost, trying to fathom His words to me. He was right about my ledger; my early successes gave me a sense of entitlement, and I took much more from the people who gave me so much. My later years I did not take as much, but I did not give back much either. Now, I'm a kinder, giving person, but I still owe.

What did He mean by "beyond what I'm thinking now?" Who beyond my six ghosts?

I began the rosary again, this time adding a prayer for this answer.

Chapter Nine

I needed to get out of the house. My ability to concentrate is based on being alone and quiet somewhere. I recently had a brain scan which concluded I have a mild form of Attention Deficit Disorder which restricts my ability to comprehend and concentrate. I always knew I was closer to Forest Gump than Albert Einstein regarding brain power, but after I was read the test's conclusions, it made sense that I took this condition for granted. Now, "tell me something I don't know" is the feeling I have.

I left a note on the kitchen table for Genna that I was going out for breakfast, and would be back in a couple of hours. I could hear her snoring in the bedroom; she probably had a couple of dreams to go before waking. There were a couple of bagels in the fridge and some egg salad which she prefers to spread anyway.

The sun, after giving me my wakeup call earlier, was eclipsed by nasty storm clouds gliding over the area. I stopped at the breakfast café in a nearby strip mall and ordered a fried egg on an English muffin and orange juice, to go. I sat in the car with the radio off, ate at a rate more quickly than I'm always chastised for, and headed off to the SAC. If I needed to think of a bigger solution, I was going to do it away from the Ark. The trip reminded me of what a nightmare Route 20 usually is, which I had been able to avoid lately, until today. It was just as well; the rhythmic cadence of the wipers was like a 'white noise' to other sounds.

What did He mean by "beyond?" Beyond the six from '71? Beyond all the former player alums? Beyond the college?

That must be it, I thought to myself. In theory, we could start something that would have a ripple effect that would make a lot more than just six people happy. In terms of effort, I thought of Kevin Costner in the movie, *Tin Cup*. He took a lot of shots before he finally aced that hole.

I had to frame this in my head in a few days before our meeting with the AD and the Coach. The traffic had eased after I got past the Route 5 exit, and in short order I was zipping over the Nemacole River and into the blue parking lot next to the SAC. The rain had eased to a sprit, so I turned the wipers and engine off, and stared at the edifice before me. How uninspiring and without a soul, I thought. The inside was different; not too many visiting teams relished playing here, its cavern of noise made it difficult to think or perform well. However, the outside design rarely made anyone happy except the concrete company who poured it. This was probably a mistake to come here for a vision of the future.

Larry Dariani had plans to change the facility in a big way, however. These I've heard would include more seating, restaurants, stores to purchase memorabilia, luxury box seating, and of course, a facelift. This is all Big. It's the time to think Big. I became anxious to hear from Ken.

The phone rang. It's Genna.

"Where are you?"

"I went to Kathy's Koffee, I drove around a bit, thinking of Back Court matters (half a fib). I was just starting back home. Anything you want to do today?"

"I have to go for a checkup, did you forget?"

"Yes, do you want me to drive you?"

"No, I'll be fine."

Genna had a health crisis not too long ago, which she has to monitor periodically, but she's feeling fine now. Either of us, or sometimes both of us, forget about it, except she tends to tire easily from daily medication she has to take. Still, I felt badly for not looking at the calendar before bolting out of the house.

"I'll be home in a half hour, if you change your mind."

When I got back home, Genna was almost ready to leave. She again declined my offer, saying it was just some routine blood work, some questions with her doctor, and a prescription refill.

"Can I take you to Pizzelli's when you get home? How about some of their linguine with white clam sauce?"

"Sounds good, but let me see how I feel when I get home. Maybe we can just have it delivered if I'm not up to going there."

"OK. Call me when you're on your way back."

She nodded, kissed my cheek, and was off in the Lexus.

I went back upstairs to the computer to send Ken an email.

"Ken, we're not thinking Big enough. This needs to go beyond the Back Court, the former players, the College, right to the NCAA. I'll lay it all out when we have our meeting." John.

* * *

"I'm on my way back. Everything's good; blood work's good. Red cells are up, must be your steaks, John. I'm up for Pizzelli's. I'll see you in about an hour."

She seemed upbeat about the visit. We'd gotten used to good reports, but you never know, and it's always a rush when they're over with. I went to the garage fridge to make sure I had a bottle of her favorite Russian River Chardonnay to bring with us.

I looked out on the deck and noticed the rain earlier in the day had dried, so I decided to wait for Genna while getting some extra vitamin D. I leaned back on the lounge chair, closed my eyes and absorbed the heat and yellow orange glow that was my favorite sign of peace. It was getting near late afternoon, but again it was twilight time for me. I could feel with my closed eyes the sun dappling over the tops of the trees, mixing a light brown with yellow orange inside my lids. There wasn't peace on earth, but for the moment, it was in my back yard.

I heard the sliding door open to the deck. I dozed for about an hour? Genna appeared with her best big smile, and bent over to kiss me.

"I'll be ready in five minutes."

Eric, the owner, greeted us at the door to the restaurant. I gave him my customary query, "Are you sure you're not Italian?" Eric would always laugh at this, because he's Jewish, and of no descent from Italy. However, he had all the sauces recipied to a tee. I decided to come up with a new joke the next time we visited, though.

We thoroughly enjoyed the two huge plates of linguine washed down with the Chard.

"Let me guess what we want for dessert. Zeppoles?" I said.

"Bingo"

Zeppoles are a much better version of warm donut holes. Eric serves them, too many of them to eat at one sitting, with powdered sugar, and a melted chocolate dip. Talk about dying and going to heaven.

We paid the check, gave Eric a hug, and rolled home in ten minutes.

"That was fun," Genna said. "I'm a little tuckered out, though. In the old days, we'd go to a movie now. Soon I'd like to see that new Woody Allen movie while it's still in theaters."

I agreed. *Midnight in Paris* was another home run by him after hitting a single with his last effort. I still would see anything by him; his creativity never ceasing to amaze.

"We'll go in a couple of days," I said.

After I took my small handful of P.M. supplements, I went to the family room to see Genna reading her book, her feet propped up on an ottoman. I flopped down in the matching chair and ottoman. I knew for certain she would be dozing off in about fifteen minutes; she was tired from the day, and she had just taken her once a day pill which makes her drowsy.

I put my head back and started to dwell on how my life became so surreal over the past few days. What made me start thinking about the Ark? There was no voice at that point that said, "Go to the Ark." Only the tug of reminiscence got me there in the first place; only then was I drawn deeper into this wormhole. I thought back to my desperate time in 1971, at wit's end trying to decide what to do with my life. That evening in early February of that year, while flipping the old channel dial in the pre-digital world, would change my life forever, and start to incur the debt which I now owed. The old channel dial that had an Ultra High Frequency between channels two and thirteen. Until that night, I was unaware that any video existed in that realm. That night the channel flip was slow enough for me to catch a glimpse of hardwood. I fine tuned and jiggled the rabbit ear antennas to hear and see Sunny Men's Basketball in progress on the court of the old Ark. This portal which closed back then had now reopened, and was offering me a chance at redemption. If I had given as much as I should have, I would just owe these guys. To settle my accounts, I had to make it better for a lot more people, past and future.

I looked over at Genna, and she was asleep. She couldn't possibly be dreaming as intensely as what's happening to me. As daunting a task as I was faced with, I was still being given a second chance. Maybe *A Christmas Carol* really did happen to someone like Scrooge. I wondered if Dickens or W.P. Kinsella, who wrote *Shoeless Joe* (later to become the *Field of Dreams* movie), went through a journey like mine. Who's to say "No," especially if they're not to tell anyone? Life is filled with second chances, and I don't think everyone that gets them does so without some sort of prodding.

Chapter Ten

A couple of days went by before I got an email from Ken confirming the AD and the Coach wanted to meet us that coming Monday at 10 A.M. at the SAC. It was the end of the week when the email arrived, so I knew what I'd be thinking about Saturday and Sunday.

The key in my mind to this meeting was the AD, Larry Dariani. Having gone to Sunny, his heart got a much better tug from tradition than Coach Wheaton, who schooled elsewhere, in Chicago. On the other hand, he prefers to be a hands-off manager. He likes to hire good people, give them the ball to run with unimpeded, or at least until they screwed up. So far, Manny Wheaton had done everything right to even the casual fan, and especially Larry.

In terms of stature, I can best describe Larry as Tom Buchanan from *The Great Gatsby*, with a brain. He's about 6' 3" 220 lbs, and looks like he could still suit up for the baseball team, which he played for in the Eighties. He was a journeyman who backed up the star player in center field, but he did get his share of playing time, and a couple of round trips home after clearing the fences. Unlike Buchanan, he didn't have a wealthy background, rather a solid middle class family who instilled a hard work ethic. A scholar-athlete at a school like Sunny puts in 18 to 20 hour days, which he did gladly, and it paid off later. Although he didn't have a pro baseball career, he was able to parlay succeeding jobs in radio, then TV, as an announcer. When the Athletic Directorship position opened at Sunny, he was in the perfect position with his back- ground to take over. Sunny, like many schools, saw their state and federal revenue support drying up, so Larry's connections with media advertisers could provide the needed funds to bridge the gap.

His demeanor is best described as between a drill sergeant and a schmoozer. He has close cropped dark hair barely starting to gray, and his ramrod posture exudes confidence and respect. His quick smile and engaging personality makes you want to be in the picture with him.

I had met him a couple of times, but with all the people he deals with even on a daily basis, I wasn't sure he would remember those encounters. This meeting from his standpoint might best be handled on a first time basis. I was still curious why Coach Wheaton wanted this meeting with Larry present. It could be good or bad. Coach could be thinking, "This is a great idea, don't you think, Larry," and we could get joint approval on the spot; or he could say, "This doesn't matter, winning is what does," then piss on the both of us in front of Larry.

The small mental wager I placed was on the former.

* * *

Saturday was uneventful. I spent the day doing a few odd jobs around the house, none of them escalating into a major project. I had to replace a toilet float. I don't know about the rest of you, but I usually just have to sniff near a plumbing chore, and it becomes very costly. This time, I didn't snap the arm, nor cause a leak or overflow. I semi-cleaned out the garage, and putzed around in my garden; and gave the plants a dose of Miracle Gro.

Genna had agreed earlier in the day to see *Midnight in Paris* that night, which was playing at a small Art Cinema in Red Shoals .

What a gem!

I don't want to spoil it for you, but it's about a writer, played by Owen Wilson, who does a fairly good job of channeling Woody in his younger days. He's struggling in Paris to finish his novel, where each night at twelve, a smoke sputtering vintage car with a 1920's literary figure inside picks him up, and through these interactions he's inspired. As clever as it all was, I thought, here's another time traveler like myself. We had great fun, and I risked cracking another molar on a bag of popcorn.

Sunday, I got another email from Ken.

"John, I've got lots of stuff I want to go over about the BC during the meeting tomorrow. For instance, I want to get approval to have a membership sign up table at some of the Football games, a BC banner to be hung at the SAC, a BC web site, a new tee shirt design logo, and some more things. Where are you going with the push for alumni participation? I don't quite see where you're going with the NCAA. Care to share?" Ken.

"Ken, I've got it all pretty straight in my head. I think you'll like what I have to say. Your agenda is very good also." John.

Ken is a cautious guy. He's always afraid of upsetting or offending someone ahead of time. Remembering how he seemed a bit intimidated by the Coach, I decided to have my remarks premier at the meeting. I'm a "let it fly" kind of guy, and that's what I was going to do.

"Good morning, John, did you have breakfast yet?"

Genna's so cute. She was calling from the kitchen, where she could see there were no dirty pots or dishes.

"How about eggs sunny side, toast, and bacon?" I shot back. "I'll be down in a minute. Make your coffee in the meantime, and put water on for my tea."

Ten minutes later, I served us with a smile, thanks to precooked bacon, which takes twenty seconds. Salt and pepper on her egg, pepper and tobasco on mine. When I was finished with my egg, I drained the bag from my cup of Tazo Zen green tea, slurp sipping to cool it off.

"What are your plans today, Genna?"

"After I watch a couple of news shows, I think I'll catch some rays on the deck while reading my book, and you?"

"I've got this meeting tomorrow morning with Ken, the AD, and the basketball coach. There are some important things I want to say, and I want to think them through. Not that you're a noise maker, but I think I'll go to the library, or someplace quiet, to mull over what I want to say."

I didn't want to say I was going to the Ark. Genna can raise her eyebrow like Vivian Leigh did in *Gone with the Wind*, and I really didn't want to see that suspicious look of hers. However, that was where I was off to (half fib, it should be quiet on a Sunday).

"You'll be home for supper, right? I'll pick up something readymade at the Italian store. Give me a hint."

"Surprise me. Whatever you feel like having." If I had to guess, we'd be having one of their fish filets, rice balls, and broccoli and oil with roasted garlic. We basically like the same foods, so I knew she wouldn't disappoint.

Within an hour, I was off to the Ark to see my apparitions. After not seeing them for a couple of days, another pep talk might be needed. Besides, I wanted to bounce a couple of thoughts about the meeting tomorrow.

I pulled into the parking lot, and was surprised to see only three cars. I surmised that on a Sunday, in the middle of the summer, there wasn't a lot going on. The campus had grown so much since I was an undergrad that the Ark wasn't in need so much as in my day. There were so many other venues that could accommodate all types of events.

Walking towards the back door, I wondered if Slick had unlocked it for me. As I got close to the door, I heard a click, but did not see anyone in the door pane. I quietly opened the door, and literally, didn't see a soul in the cavernous space. I walked briskly towards the supply room door, in case that watchman was prowling his beat.

I opened the door slowly, remembering the hinges needed some oil. Leaning against the table was someone I didn't expect.

John

John Bird was the freshman center on the team. I was expecting to see Slick.

"Where are the rest of the guys, John?"

"They're in the lounge. I was the one who let you in. I was hoping you'd be back soon, because I wanted to say a few things."

"John, you didn't even know I was coming today. How did you unlock the door before I got to it?"

"We all have a sense when you are approaching the building. We don't have to look out the window; we can just feel your approach. It's sort of like feeling a wind when a weather front is near."

I couldn't help but notice his body language. Because of his 6' 9" frame, he was more sitting than leaning on the table. His huge hands that could palm a basketball with only three fingers gripped the edge of the table, with the fingers tapping the underside nervously. During the short time I had been there, he crossed and uncrossed his long legs twice.

"John," I said, "you can tell me whatever's on your mind. I can tell you, your shyness will go away soon enough."

I was alluding to the fact that it was painful to watch him interview his freshman year, but the year after and onwards, his mouth grew a megaphone. It was refreshing to watch him come into his own with confidence.

He shrugged, picked his chin off his chest, and looked at me.

"I'm really worried about Charlie. That little pep talk you gave us a few days ago helped him a little, but he just looks so pained all the time. That year we played, he was like a father to me. I never could have played at the level I did as a freshman if he wasn't looking out for me. He just had a set of wings that season; he just flew on and off the court. He still plays like he used to, but between games he looks like a big dodo bird about to become extinct. We all feel we're here for him, mostly. We all feel there's something missing, and there are holes in our hearts; but his heart, you could put your fist through."

"Mr. Bird, tomorrow the shit hits the fan. I'm meeting with the AD and the coach, with the hope of helping you guys first, but in so doing, a lot of other people. You guys are just the tip of the iceberg. If I succeed, there will be far more meaning to what you guys did that year, I promise. If CB doesn't want to talk now, I understand; but you tell him what I'm about to do started with him."

He seemed to take it in, but his demeanor didn't seem to change.

"Can I make a suggestion?" I said, "As a change of pace, why don't you guys go jump in the pool; it'll do you good."

"We don't feel we can. It's hard to explain. We have a fear of that pool. A couple of times, we went into the pool room, and none of us could jump in. It was like we couldn't take another step. We've stopped trying."

This was a hard one to figure out. They all take showers. Are ghosts allergic to chlorine? It would be a perfect thing to lessen the boredom that they, especially Charlie, were feeling.

"Maybe because swimming isn't basketball related. Wish me luck."

I quietly backtracked through the back door, and sat in the car nearly motionless for thirty minutes. The gears between my ears were turning, though. My thoughts about the meeting dropped into the right order, and I said to myself what Frank Lloyd Wright said to his *Fallingwater* client: I'm ready for you. I started the engine and began weaving the Eos around the side streets to Route 20, and home.

* * *

Genna had the table set when I got home about mid afternoon. On Sundays growing up, both of us with Italian mothers were always served dinner around 3:30 P.M. Even though ours were not such elaborate affairs, we still kept the time slot.

"Wait 'til you see what I got us."

I watched as she punched the microwave to run for two minutes. Out came our two plates of baked flounder with what looked like a franchaise sauce, a rice ball stuffed with ricotta cheese, and broccoli with oil and garlic.

"How's that look?"

I did my best to look pleased and surprised; hoping she would settle for pleased.

We suffered when we first moved to New Castle County from Bergen County, New Jersey, where there was a very good Italian store every other block, until we found Tuscano's on Route 9, which opened about six months ago. We tried one store after another before Tuscano's opened, and they all weren't what we were used to. Once again, this entrée tasted home-made.

"What are you going to do after you clean up?" Genna said as she gave me that little payback smirk of hers.

"I'll probably cruise my streaming Netflix, and try a four star rated film I've never heard of. I'm off to bed after that; I've got that meeting tomorrow, remember?"

"OK. I'm going to read some more, but I might give "60 Minutes" a try, then I'll read some more. I started that new David McCullough book, *The Greater Journey*. It's a great book. He's a very good historic story teller. It's about a group of writers, artists, and professional people like doctors and architects who went to Paris in the 1830's to around the turn of the century to study their fields. At that time, Paris was at the vanguard of culture and science, not New York or anywhere else in the US. He points out that while the western movement was taking place in this country for the masses, culture and science was going the other way. It's fascinating; you should read it after me."

The book did sound interesting to me, but I was hung up on the title, and thinking of my "greater journey" starting tomorrow at 10 A.M.

I did find another good indie film to stream called *Arranged.* It's about two young women, one Muslim, the other a Jew, whose families are each trying to arrange marriages for them. It all works out, and they become friends for life, once again begging the question: Why can't we all just get along?

It was twilight time again. That same old feeling.

Chapter Eleven

I got up around six, and walked and prayed more briskly than usual. During breakfast cereal, I did the crossword puzzle very quickly, since it is the easiest on Monday. I left the house at nine, believing I would miss the rush hour. Being correct, I arrived at the SAC at 9:40. I saw Ken's car and pulled alongside his.

"Good morning, John, are you ready for this?"

He seemed a little jittery, and when I said, "Yes, I am. You go first."

That didn't seem to calm him down.

"Ken, this isn't going to be the end of the world. Whatever the outcome, we'll be able to gauge what level of involvement they expect out of the Back Court. We'll hear their concerns, if any, and we'll deal with them, that's all."

"Let's do it," I added.

I had never been in any of the offices at the SAC, yet my first visit was at the top, the AD's. It was what I had expected. Larry's appearance was on the Spartan side, nothing very flashy. He seemed inclined to dress sporty casual. In most pictures I've seen of him he's wearing a blazer and jeans, although the jeans obviously don't come from the Gap store.

His office had the same flavor; a plain desk and chair, and there were no furnishings that you would describe as plush. The most striking feature of the office was the number of photos, seemingly touching each other so it was hard to tell the paint color on the wall. I didn't dwell on looking at any of them, because I didn't want to get distracted, or seem star-struck. I just assumed there were numerous luminaries from the world of sports before and during his directorship.

Ken and I just looked at Larry and Coach Wheaton as they both got up to shake hands. Each had a slight smile, not the kind like they just won something.

Larry spoke first, "Ken, John, it's good to see you guys. We asked you up here because although you have some good new ideas, we're not totally sold. We want you two to close the sale, convince us that these ideas can be implemented and sustained through the Back Court."

Ken looked at me and launched into his spiel. He detailed the new initiatives to drive up membership, from having a larger presence at football games with a membership sign up table; for the first time, a BC website, which would be essentially a blog with a sign up app. Ken really cruised into the new tee shirt design, and coordinating the sale of signed memorabilia at auction. Ken had a little P. T. Barnum in him; he was a born promoter.

When he finished, Larry and Manny appeared to be impressed.

Coach said to Ken, "Nice presentation, and I'm impressed. Larry, I'd like to do everything he's suggested, if it's OK with you. What I really want to hear is from you, John, about your proposal regarding the former players. That I think can get really complicated, and may not even be necessary. We were able to sell the program this year with zip to go on, and we're going to put a winner on the court this year. So go ahead, make me buy what you're selling."

I now understood why we were having this meeting with the AD present. Coach really didn't want to get that involved with former players, or the history and tradition of the program, at least at this time. Maybe he was on overload as Karen, his wife suggested. I made a compelling argument at the Ark meeting, which he couldn't say no to out of hand, and then risk being overrode by Larry on appeal.

I glanced over at Ken and then Larry. I took a slow deep breath and began.

"Coach, the other goal of the Back Court is not short term, like the initiatives that Ken has described. His part of the plan is a booster shot to the fan base, a B_{12} to energize them. They're essential, and they have to be modified or added to each year to stay fresh. Just like your recruiting, each class hopefully builds on the success of the previous year's efforts."

"What I'm proposing is a long term plan to insure the success and stability of the program you're building. I don't know you all that well, coach, but my gut tells me you're a clean coach; you don't cut corners, you play by the rules. You're not like that other guy, who's name will go unmentioned here, that built power house programs in a short time, then left those programs just ahead of the sanctions imposed by the NCAA when they caught up with what was going on, and he's done this three or four times."

The other three in the room chuckled or smirked, knowing exactly who I was speaking of.

"That's not you, coach. I know Larry, and he wouldn't hire someone like that. Getting these alums involved will help yours and our program in several ways. First, they're good will ambassadors in their communities, and they know talent. What's wrong with having an unlimited number of scouts on the recruiting trail? That helps you, and it helps us by increasing our membership in the BC. You know that most fans are groupies at heart; they love to schmooze with old and new players alike."

"To this point, the BC will do the reaching out. We'll write the letters and correspondence, for your approval, of course. The athletic office will just have to do the mailings, to keep the alum's confidentiality. We expect interest to grow slowly at first, probably a function of our sincerity, and your success on the court, since everybody loves a winner."

Another round of smirks.

"Here's the other reason why we should be doing this. It's the right thing to do. I'll repeat for Larry's benefit what I said to you at the Ark. These players are not boxes of Kleenex that last for three or four years, then are tossed away empty. They put a lot more in the coffers of the schools they represent than the amount of scholarship money paid to them. The colleges, universities, and certainly the NCAA benefit big time. Larry and Manny, wouldn't you like to run a business like the NCAA that pays out virtually a minimum wage, and makes billions? I would."

"Doing the right thing here is a way to turn the situation to our advantage. Bringing these former players back can allow them to network for career opportunities, and they can give back by mentoring younger players. The BC will be the CPU of this new database that will form. This would be another way of looking at the term "booster club." I'm not suggesting that the Back Court or the college become an employment agency, but whatever we can do to get these guys to the inside of the track, we should do. If this gets going like I know it will, we can hold this up to the NCAA as a model that says, 'This is what you should be doing."

I was making constant eye contact between Larry and Manny, and so far, no sign of my convincing either.

"Coach, I'm sure we in the Back Court are going to have to learn by making mistakes as we go, just as you did this past year as a coach."

This got his attention even more, and his gaze lasered on mine more intently.

"You took your lumps with the referees the past year, being a new coach in the toughest league, with the most future hall of fame coaches to compete against. You yelled and screamed at them, as if they were your players, working for you. The stat sheets of three or four close games had many more fouls called on Sunny than the opposition. But in that final game of the season, which we all know was slanted toward the other team advancing in the tournament, you took the high road at the press conference, which earned the refs' respect, so they marked your dues "paid in full." My guess is Larry suggested you do that, but you agreed. You're going to get those close calls this year."

Larry and Manny looked at each other like, "How'd he guess that?"

I wanted to turn and talk directly to Larry, but knew I had to stay on Manny. I rounded the clubhouse turn, and gave him my final sprint to the finish.

"Coach, let's give this a shot. Not too long ago, we had a lot more former player involvement, and the excitement in the fan base was electric. The SAC had so much more juice, other teams hated to come here, and we beat some pretty good teams with less talent than you're putting on the floor now."

The moment came that I least expected, but welcomed anyway. Larry, who had been stoic, without giving as much as a nod during my spiel, cut in.

"Manny, I think John's right. I know what he was talking about a few years ago, two coaches ago to be precise. What he's proposing has an upside, and really no downside. Let's let the BC run with this, too."

Coach nodded his assent, but I could tell he wasn't all that enthusiastic. It could be the stress his wife alluded to during this time of the approaching season. Or, I thought more likely, he was used to being in full control of all matters in his program. Larry probably gave him that in the hotel room on day one of his pitch for the head coaching position.

Anyway, I didn't care. I just got by him, and was able to drive to the basket. I would have to prove I was right on this to win him over, but that's OK.

Larry stood up from behind his desk, signaling we were just about done, and said,

"Why don't you guys draft a letter, send it up to us for approval, and we'll get this started?"

Ken chimed in, "John's a writer, in fact he's writing his first book, and so he'll do the draft."

Larry inquired what the book was about.

"I can't tell you that. It's bad luck." I said.

We all shook hands, and Ken and I thanked them for their time. Coach just glanced at me quickly as he shook my hand, and left the room.

Ken and I turned to leave, when I heard Larry say:

"John, good job."

* * *

"You hit a three pointer, but I had to drive hard for my layup," I said to Ken as we left the AD's office and walked towards our cars in the lot. Needless to say, we were all smiles.

"You made the shot, got fouled, and made the free throw, so we both scored three," Ken joked. We both had elation levels high enough to laugh hysterically at this, a rather lame joke at any other time.

"You have time for me to buy you a burger at Raffael's? We can get in before the lunch mob if we go now," I said.

"I'll see you there, but I'm buying," Ken countered.

"Since I had to work harder, you're on!" We sped off; he following, as I thought of a pint of Bass out of a new keg.

I guessed right about the lunch hour. Ten minutes after we were seated, the place was mobbed. We both smiled again as I clinked my Bass to his Irish Red. Every time I have Bass ale, I think of the worst maritime disaster, the HMS *Titanic*; not only for the loss of life, but also for the ten thousand cases of Bass that went down with it.

"I had NO idea what you were going to say, but you sure did pull it off. Nice job."

"Actually, Larry pulled it off. Everything I said was directed at him, although I was looking and talking to the coach. As a former student athlete at the Sunny, I knew Larry would realize most others weren't as fortunate to have the success that he has. I hoped if I hit enough bells and whistles, he would chime in like he did. Notice I didn't bring up the Champ team specifically. I'm still doing this for them, but they're part of the bigger picture now."

"Is it me, or wasn't the coach too happy when he left the office?" I added.

"I think he's very protective about his control over HIS program, but once he sees the idea is successful, he'll be on board like that," Ken snapped his fingers for emphasis.

"Can I take your orders?" a hostess with the mostess queried, trying to charm a man and his son (or so she thought), to maximize her tip later.

"Ken, two cheddar burger specials, and another round?"

"Sounds good."

She sauntered away like a runway model, and we got back to business.

"I'll get started on the letter tonight. Hopefully after they rework the draft, we can send it out around the end of August."

"Since it's your idea, would you be willing to be the contact person for the alums as they respond?"

"Sure," I said.

We talked, and talked, and talked. As I said before, Ken really had a feel for this stuff. He devoted virtually all his free time to the basketball program. Also, he must have the most understanding boss ever. Ken takes the schedule of games for the coming season, as soon as he gets it, to his boss, who lets Ken arrange his days off and vacations around the home AND away games. He's missed one game, due to a snowstorm, in ten years. If there's a fine line between dedication and obsession, Ken knows how to walk it.

We finished our burgers and second round pints. He paid the check as promised, gave Miss Model Waitress a nice, but standard tip, which provoked an eye roll and a curt thank you as she left the table.

"Thanks again, Ken. We'll talk tonight on the internet."

I walked to my car in the parking deck around the corner. I had let Ken have the last space in front of Raffael's when we pulled up for lunch. I considered going back to the Ark, to give the ghosts an update, but decided not to. I sat there, and started to compose the letter in my head. I thought again about Frank Lloyd Wright; how he wouldn't put a plan to paper until it was clear in his head. I hoped for a letter like his plan for *Fallingwater*, just from the standpoint of having an impact. If it had that kind of impact, I would need to worry about the logistics of answering quite a few responses, as Ken asked me to do.

But I was getting ahead of myself; I'd better just get back to the letter.

I began to wonder how long this effort would take to be meaningful, for Coach Wheaton to "be on board," as Ken put it.

ADD again. I'd better just get back to the letter.

* * *

I got the call just as I was getting onto Route 20 once again, while twirling a few words in my head.

"John, Donna and I are going over to the new Costco to check it out, and then we'll probably get a bite for supper around there. You're on your own. How did the meeting go?"

"Great, they agreed to let us do what we want. It's a new day for the Back Court and Sunny basketball."

We hung up, and I decided to skip going home, instead continued down Route 20 to Baybury Park. In forty-five minutes I arrived and lucked out with a parking space near Il Cuchina restaurant on the ocean. I walked onto the boardwalk between the restaurant and the rusting hulk of the Arcade just south of it. I found it strange how two towns so close in Delaware resembled two towns near the New Jersey shore where I spent so much time as a kid. First Long Beach and Long Branch, now Baybury and Asbury Park, seemed so similar in appearance. The salty sea and mist had savaged this Arcade structure, just like the one in Asbury, making it sad for anyone with a history there to witness. I turned my back on the Arcade, walked north a few short blocks, and found a bench to sit on. I began to imagine that I was in Asbury Park.... I propped myself on the bench in such a way that I could trade glances at the ocean, and imagined the Stone Pony club just to my left....

The Stone Pony was simply a world renowned Mecca to rock and roll, and more importantly to the locals as the main proponent of the "Jersey" sound. It is a magical, almost sacred place on Earth for what it is. Springsteen, Southside Johnny, Bon Jovi, and many others brought and received energy from the venue. Despite the megawatts emanating from it in this millennium, there was a time in the 90's when its spirit was lost, and the Pony almost died. Could the Ark be like the Pony, and recharge the lives of many?

The white noise of the wind and surf, and the inspiration of a resurrected musical icon seemed to be a good spot to summon a new spirit for my life. Spirit is energy, and I wanted to provide more of it.

I spent another hour on that bench, mostly for the calming effect the sea renders to body and soul.

In a snap, I remembered I wasn't in Asbury Park, New Jersey.

I returned home to an empty, quiet house, and hoped Genna would keep it that way by not returning for a few hours.

The draft I sent Ken recapped everything I had said both times I had confronted the Coach with my proposal. I must admit, it was a pretty good sales pitch to entice the alums to give us another look. I spoke of energy, fun, refreshments, free membership, (based on their previous toils on the hardwood), before getting around to networking and mentoring. I attached a basic questionnaire to get feedback from them to gauge whether we were on the right track.

"John, I think the draft will get approval with minor changes. We're off and running," Ken.

* * *

The letter went out to the former players from the basketball office in the beginning of September. As I suspected, the responses started dribbling in at a slow rate. Football season was just starting, and the basketball season was still a good two months away. Since I was the contact person for the BC, I got the email responses from the players. If they provided a phone number, I gave them a follow up call to personally invite them to the next BC meeting held the first week of November. Otherwise, I email a reply to them with the information.

A response I was really waiting for came the third week in September. It was from Slick Sampson. Hearing from a "former" ghost was the main part of my effort. Since I didn't directly appeal for them to be recognized before the end of the year 2011, this was another one of my "back door" plays to get them their due.

As I mentioned before I had met Slick from time to time over the years, so I knew more of his post Sunny history than the others on that team.

"Slick, it's great to hear from you. You're going to take up our offer?"

"Yeah, John, I would like to. I've been pretty bummed out about the program the last few years …"

"You and me both," I cut in on his thought. "I just want to forget they ever happened. There were mistakes made all around. The former coach was not enough of a manager to put the program all together. His level of frustration his last couple of years regarding this was hard for all of us to bear. That's over now, and he and we have moved on. I wish him well, and he's not a bad person."

"Slick, let me ask you something else. Are you also bummed out that your team's fortieth anniversary slipped by in silence?"

"Yes and no, John. It would have been nice, but I understand coaches have their own agendas. Besides, equaling our feat of thirty-four straight wins is highly unlikely, and he has maybe two or three years to get it done or get out. If he wanted to use the winning streak or the Champ appearance as goals for his team, that would be OK, too."

"Slick, I have an idea. I haven't seen you in a while. Why don't we meet at the old Ark? We can shoot the breeze some more, and I'll buy you a beer at that little pub around the corner. What do you say? I'll tell you, I've been back to the Ark a few times recently, and it's still a magical place."

He had no idea.

"I'm game, John. How's tomorrow night sound?"

'You're on, and you can tell me how Candice's doing." I mentioned Slick's daughter before. She was one of the best female college basketball players to ever touch a ball. I would love to have an update on her plans.

"She's fine. I'll see you tomorrow, around 7 P.M?"

I detected a definite tone of voice change after I asked about his daughter.

"See you then, Slick. I'll meet you at the back door at the northwest corner."

There would be activity at the Ark at that hour, I was sure. However, if the door was locked, I wondered who would open it this time. Also, Slick suggested we meet the following night, which I took to mean he was placing a priority on the meeting, for whatever reason.

* * *

I arrived first at the Ark, around 6:45, my fifteen minute early window kicking in again. I stood outside the door waiting. Just inside the door, someone else was waiting; I didn't have to guess who. My back was turned to the door, and he seemed puzzled why I wasn't entering. Trusting his lip reading ability, I mouthed that I was meeting someone.

Was he in for a surprise.

Slick arrived about ten minutes later. I hadn't seen him for a few years, but he still looked the same, like he could suit up and still play. As I said before, he had a deadly perimeter shot, before the three pointer was instituted in college basketball. I remembered at that last meeting, I had him going with one of my dead pan jokes:

"Slick,' I said, "What do you think of the new NCAA rule that's been proposed?"

"Which one is that?"

"Well, they're proposing that each college team can appoint a former player who suits up, and sits on the bench most of the game, but, if the situation arises, that player can step on the court, receive a long pass, take a shot, then sit back down. If it goes in, its FOUR points. Would you be up for something like that?"

For about two seconds after the question mark, I had him, and then he burst out laughing.

No shit, if they did come up with that rule, he would be an asset.

"Hey, John, how are you?"

He usually said 'hey' instead of 'hi'.

"I'm good, and glad you could make it. Let's step inside onto your old playground."

He smiled and chuckled, but that's exactly what it was to those team members; they toyed and played with every opponent on this court that year.

When we went inside, there were two separate games of intramural basketball going on, which when I was a gym rat undergrad, I did on a regular basis. I was glad to see, to eliminate further confusion, the vintage 1971 Sunny and Megamont teams were not playing at that time. We walked around the perimeter of the court and watched the mediocre effort on either end for a short time. I pointed to a spot near the half court and side line and said:

"Look, there's where you and Quincy mercilessly stole the ball, and took turns padding your scoring averages."

Another chuckle.

"John, there's a small supply room down the far end where we can probably talk without interruption."

"I know it well."

We went into the room, and not being surprised again, there was the Slick model 1971 leaning against the wall, his chin dropping almost to his chest when he noticed who I had met outside.

"Slick ..."

"John, please call me Reece, my given name. Not too many people call me Slick anymore. I've lost most of the moves and quickness that got me the nickname in the first place."

"Reece, as in Reece "Goose" Tatum? You remind me of him, also." Tatum was one of the original Harlem Globetrotters, who could have played with anybody.

"Reece it is," I added. However, to myself I still wanted to call him Slick. I would try to remember when I spoke to him directly. Glancing over at the wall, I could see the earlier version of Reece preferred Slick also.

"Reece," I began again, "I guess you could see how serious we are in the Back Court about this endeavor. We really want to assist the former players' concerns in any way we can. Is there any area of your current situation that we can help you with?"

"Well John, I've had a series of jobs related to personnel or office management, and although those jobs aren't going to make me or anybody rich, I've generally enjoyed working with people. I' m happy to have A job in this economy."

"Reece, I can't tell you I can pick up the phone right now, and hook you up with another alum who's a titan of industry that will double your salary, but that's the kind of connectivity we eventually want to establish. We want the college, with everything else being equal, to help its own first. Obviously, the network is small at this point, but as we get going, the BC will manage the data, and the meetings can become job conventions of a sort. Start coming to the meetings, and there's a fair chance you'll be able to upgrade your position down the road."

I could see he agreed with all of this, but I sensed there was something else there to talk about. I'm not a prying person, but I jumped on this one.

"Reece, what else would you like to talk about? I'm a good listener, and it won't go out of this room."

He hesitated, took a deep breath, and let out as deep a sigh.

"It's Candy, my daughter. It's a tough time for us. Her mother and I divorced years ago; I was there with the monetary support, but not the emotional. Her mother did a wonderful job raising Candice, and she doesn't take sides between our daughter and me. I was there for Candy when she started to show skills for the game, but not much before. We haven't been in touch for a couple of years. She hasn't come out and said it, but I think she feels I only came around when I saw bushels of money over her horizon. I don't quite know how to get around this. I'm hoping for a second chance at being a good father to her, and for her to know I'm for real. I don't want her money; I just want my daughter back."

The words “second chance” leapt out at me.

Slick and I were looking for the same thing.

“Reece, I think you will get that chance. For now, tell her that even though you weren’t in the past, you’re there for her NOW, 24/7. Make the call, and don’t stop until she talks to you. Make it clear that you owe her, not the other way around, and also make that clear to her mother, who Candy must be closer to, regardless how things were in the past. Open a new chapter in your lives, just like we’re doing at the BC.”

All the while I’m saying this; the young transparent guy leaning against the wall is “spooked,” like he’s seeing the ghost of Christmas future. I wasn’t planning on spooking a ghost, but I did.

“Reece, remember, this is a new chapter all around. I hope I helped.”

“John, you did. You were right to come to this place, it does seem magical. It’s almost like there’s a good spirit in the room with us.”

“Maybe there is. In the past, this place has been good for the both of us. Got time for that beer, and maybe a slice of pizza?”

“I’m going to take a rain check. Thanks again, though. You really took a load off me.”

“Reece, I hope to hear from your teammates, but I’d like to talk to them individually, as we just did. I hope they all contact me. If you can put in a good word …”

He smiled, “Don’t worry, I will. I don’t see them all very often, though. I’ll see you at that first meeting of the season.”

With that, the current Mr. Sampson walked out the door, and drove somewhere into the sunset.

I turned toward the 1971 version, who seemed to regain his composure.

“What happened to you while I was talking to your ‘old man’?”

"I felt if he got any closer to me, one or both of us was going to explode."

"I guess that stands to reason; both of you can't be in the same place at the same time." It seemed a plausible explanation.

"As bad as I felt then, I feel ten times better now. I feel rested and fulfilled."

"Reece, I can't tell you how good it is to hear that."

"I'm still Slick, he's Reece."

Always the joker.

"Where are your confederates?"

"Probably out on the court."

"Do you think they heard any of this?"

"No. We respect each others' privacy."

He walked through, and I walked out the door behind him. I waved to his teammates as he joined them for another tipoff. They looked at him, and then looked at me. Slick just took his place around the jump circle, and said to the ref:

"Ball up."

His body language said to them, "I don't want to talk about it."

I decided to go to Pietro's pizzeria two blocks away. I knew the place well, as it was right down the street from the fraternity I had belonged to. Root beer and pizza fueled many an all nighter while I lived at the house. Walking westward, I could see the red clouds like dying embers fading to black. The "red sky at night" adage came to mind again. Hopefully, tomorrow would fulfill a promise like today.

* * *

The pizzeria's décor had changed, having been renovated a time or two since my last visit about forty years ago. However, the plastic blue and white checked table cloths looked the same, but they added white poly coated chairs with sky blue seats that had a Sunny feel to them. The place still had that shop worn feel, and I suspected its business model was still the same: slinging pizza at a bunch of college kids feverishly in need of carbs. I walked up to the counter and ordered a slice and a root beer, for old time's sake. I moved down the counter to the stand, eat, and go section; wondering which 71'er I would hear from next.

I walked back to the Ark parking lot and decided, what the hell. I went back into the Ark to watch some more vintage hoops. The place was just about empty. I walked past a few undergrads who had wet hair; probably from doing laps in the pool. I walked past both benches into the supply room, and peered out the door's glass window to watch the action. There was about five minutes left in the half; Mega was ahead by three points. It was easy to see Slick had the most energy on the court, jawing and cursing his teammates onward. He noticed my mug in the window, and flashed that big smile of his that said, "I'm happy again."

I decided to go home at that moment. No outcome of the game was going to feel better than that smile.

Chapter Twelve

A few days later, the responses from former players began arriving at a faster rate. The season was approaching, and formal practices would start soon. There must be a subliminal urge in former players to start gearing up, at least mentally. Also, Ken really had the publicity wheels churning. The announcements and the web site had the effect of flashing lights in Las Vegas, making last year's releases seem like signs on poster board. Most of the responders were freshly minted, having recently put their stamp on the program within the last five years. However, three more 71'ers were now on the list: Harry, John, and Byron sent me their phone numbers.

Who should I call first? Harry and Byron were the closest of the three; I'd seen them together at games a few times, not just the time I confronted them with my story. John was the loner of the whole group, the one I knew least about. I'd only seen him at ten year intervals; at half time to remember the Champ achievement, and talked to briefly only once. He seemed to have the least contact with the others. I decided to call John Bird. .

I emailed the three of them, telling Harry and Byron I would call them soon. John I emailed giving him my phone number, and told him I would call the next day to set up a meeting. By having my number, I thought it would lessen the chance of him deep-sixing the call, as I am prone to do at times. If I don't recognize the number, and I don't feel like talking anyway; its two strikes and you're out.

Nine o' clock the next morning, I was able to reach him.

"John, you've made my day just by picking up the phone," I said after ID'ing myself. "I also just heard from Harry and Byron; I'm thinking Reece might have called you?"

"He did. I hadn't heard from him in quite a few years; that's probably my fault. He said, 'John, it's Reece." I said, "Who?"

"I know. I had to stand corrected after calling him 'Slick' the other night. Well, it's his call, but I still think of him as Slick, just not to his face."

"My thoughts exactly. I'm glad he was able to reach me. I live in South Carolina, and have a small farm near the town where I was born. I'm up in the Big Apple for a few days to look at some equipment at auction. I thought we could meet somewhere at night during that time."

Johnny Bird, do I know the place, I thought before saying, "John, I don't know if he told you, but I met Slick at the old Ark on Colters Avenue, where you never lost a game your freshman year. He agreed it's still a magical place; I bet you'll feel the same way. Since you'll be making the trip across the river, I'll buy you dinner at Tommy's Pub. They moved it further south down Colters Avenue since you and I were at school, but I've heard it's still pretty good. What do you say?" I also have a history at Tommy's, but more on that later.

"That'll work for me. I'm flying out of Wilmington to go home anyway. I rented a car in the Apple, and I'm driving down to the old haunt to stay with friends. I can meet you at the Ark around six tomorrow. Is that OK with you?"

"You're on, John. See you then." I also told him about the back door entrance.

It seemed to me that Slick picked up the phone very quickly after we met, and called his teammates. They had all received the letter about three weeks before. All of a sudden, I hear from three more of them in succession? Was he able to reach all of them? Quincy I could understand, he's still heavily involved in the game at the pro level, although not as a head coach, and he's out of the area also. Not hearing yet from Charlie is what I was concerned about. If I could meet and talk to only one of them, it would be him.

I joined Genna in the kitchen as she was making her standard brew.

"Would you like a soft boiled egg on an English muffin?" I asked. The wrinkled nose prompted me to try again. "On toast instead, with sausage?" Just a half wrinkle this time, before answering:

"Hold the sausage."

As I boiled the water, fed the toaster, and warmed up pre-cooked sausage for myself, I asked:

"Can I buy you lunch today at a place we haven't been for a while?"

"Where?"

"Tommy's Pub. Remember that place? Where, when we met you had lunch and dinner there on the same day?" I was alluding to the fiasco of our first blind date, when our mutual friend took her there for lunch, and I supper.

"C'mon, I'll behave this time." I tried to do everything but oink on that first date; not one of my prouder moments.

"What's the occasion?"

"No occasion, and nothing ulterior. Let's just go." I didn't want to tell her I wanted to check the place out before bringing John there the next night.

"OK, I'll be ready around five thirty or six."

That's Genna; she always leaves a window because she's always late.

After breakfast, I went back to the computer to follow up on the other responses the BC had received. At this rate, I might need help to carry the load. As I said, most of these were former players three to five years past graduation. Some of them went on to other careers right away, and others continued to play overseas until they realized they needed to find real jobs that would pay more than they were making on the court. That, plus the injury toll: a knee here, a twisted ankle there, all added up to chore and punishment, instead of fun. Welcome back guys, your dreams were you ticket out (the old *Welcome Back, Kotter* song), but you're awakening among friends. I was betting Ken couldn't wait to start promoting future meetings as to what alums would be in attendance. I tried to personalize my responses. I did have a good recall of outstanding plays over the years, and I tried to include as many of those as I could. If I couldn't match a play to a player, I tried to be the least generic as I could.

Before I knew, it was around three thirty in the afternoon. I was so absorbed, but my stomach finally got my attention around that time. I decided to call it a day with a final email to Ken, forwarding my responses, hoping he can read a lot faster than I can type.

I resorted to my quick hunger response by grabbing a few pretzels, and a ninety cal can of Coke.

"Genna, I'm going to take a shower, and get ready for our big date."

"Ha Ha!"

A while later, we arrived at Tommy's, which had the same feel inside as the old place where Genna and I had our first moment of infamy. It actually looked like they used the same weathered boards from an old farmhouse that they reassembled at this site.

I told our greeter that we had our first date at the old location almost forty three years ago.

"Really?"

Was all he said, as he spun around and marched us to a booth, plopped down two menus, and walked away without another word.

"I wasn't that cold and rude on our first date, was I?"

"No, but if you were, for sure we would have been history."

This slight was soon smoothed over by a cheery undergrad waitress, who seemed to be a walking Franz Hals portrait. She gave us time to scan the menu, which looked varied and not too pricey. However, for old time's sake, I ordered their cheeseburger with crinkle fries, and Genna ordered a shrimp salad. The burger was the two-fisted kind, and they understood what I meant by "medium." Genna enjoyed her salad, but as usual, she took half home.

As we left, we walked past the greeter, who just said:

"Bye."

He sure didn't major in personality, I thought. However, the food and the service between him were acceptable. It would be John Bird and Tommy's tomorrow night.

"I behaved much better on this date, didn't I?"

"I think I'll keep you."

"I'm glad you decided that back then."

Chapter Thirteen

I was beginning to resign myself that I had to go for a checkup regarding this twilight feeling before bedtime. I didn't want to mention it to Genna before I checked it out myself. Some nights, my eyes became very watery, even with rapid blinking; I couldn't clear the image of what I was looking at. The queasiness and floating sensation were about the same. When I finally did fall asleep and awoke, the feeling was gone, and during the day I never thought about it. It's just that I was reminded of it every evening.

Morning again. Johnny Bird day.

I eased myself out of bed, and slipped into my walking shorts and shirt. While stretching, I tried to imagine John involved with farming, much less at a tractor auction. Then again, I really didn't know much about his family, or his roots in South Carolina. I did recall that when introduced before game time, the announcer always stated a suburb of San Francisco as his hometown. Anyway, I guess I'd be catching up about him when we met.

The rest of the day was Samo, as Basquiat, the young abstract painter of the 1980's would put it. Same old, same old, not much different to report.

Soon enough, it was time to head back to the Ark. At least I didn't have to make excuses to Genna; the Back Court business covered me.

As I pulled into the lot, I noticed a black Cadillac Escalade parked near the door. I pulled up on the driver's side, and sure enough, it's John Bird, plus not many, but a few pounds. It was a little after 5:30 P.M. Either he had no traffic coming out of the city, or he really wanted to talk; or maybe neither. I waved through the windows. He got out of the car, all 6' 9" of him; as I said, with a few extra pounds.

A big smile greeted me with:

"You must be John," as his hand swallowed mine.

"Tell me, John," I said, "which car do you like better? This car or the convertible you used to tool around as a student athlete?"

"No car I ever had could replace that sky blue Caddy."

"Do you remember what you paid for that Caddy?"

He swallowed the canary, and smirked, "No, I really don't remember."

We both roared, having broken the ice.

I started in, "John, I can't tell you how important it is to the club that we hear from former players like yourself. As I said to Slick, we have a lot of ground to make up, and we don't want to just expand a social club. We want to do things that have lifetime meaning. We want to touch people, we want to pick people up, and we want to be there when needed. This is the payback we owe you."

"Why," I continued, "are we standing out here; the magic is inside." We both chuckled, and headed for the back door.

If you're 6' 9", it's hard to go unnoticed. As we walked into the Ark, John turned heads. No one knew him; just that he was tall, and probably a former player.

We walked onto center court, were John controlled many a tip. He had a knack for timing the ref's toss, to tip the ball near its top assent, before the opposing center could rise up to it. The other center often could jump higher, but John got to the ball first. I watched him scan the open space, from the rafters, to the cheap seats, and to the side lines, lost in thought.

"Is the crowd still in your ear, John?"

"Yeah, it's still there, it's almost like a recording."

"I told you there was magic here." As I said that, John Bird, circa 1971 walked through the supply room door without opening it. He had his clean home white uniform on, ready for action. Young John stopped at center court, near the out of bounds line. He must have sensed what Slick experienced the other day. It must have been akin to a silent fence for a dog. He stared intently at his modern day self.

"So John, tell me what's on your mind." I asked, glancing at the both of them.

"Looking at this old place makes me realize how far I've come in the world, but also what I've missed along the way. When I was a freshman, I couldn't handle all the attention; I had a hard time putting two sentences together in an interview."

"I remember a couple of those that first year for you. The interviewer was like a dentist pulling teeth."

"Worse than that, I actually felt I was AT the dentist, but that magnificent season made me feel I belonged playing at that level and beyond. It gave me more confidence than I needed for the rest of my life. Confidence is the difference maker in college and pro sports. Our team had the confidence and will from game one that we could and would beat anybody. That lasted until the thirty-fifth game, the Championship. We started thinking, 'Major school, big time program, etc', and the confidence was lost, as well as the game."

"After that year, I started thinking more in terms of my individual stats. I had enough confidence for myself, but I wasn't trying to make my teammates better. I just took it for granted we wouldn't go undefeated again, and I became selfish. Looking back, to this day, I regret it. If I was unselfish as I was as a freshman, we probably wouldn't have gone undefeated, but we still would have done better."

"Personally, I became selfish also. I had success in the pros, but I forgot where I came from. I got plenty of calls from my teammates, especially Charlie Bennett, but I pretty much blew them off, or had very short conversations. I was just wrong, and I've come to realize that I haven't given back enough. I made some good money in the pros, and I spent a goodly amount, also; but I still have more than I'll ever need. I owe CB big time; he was like a father to me. I'm ashamed and embarrassed, and I'm almost paralyzed to pick up the phone."

He had his head down like he was in a confession booth, and kept it there for a few moments. I glanced over at the younger version, who seemed to be taking a few deep breaths, like he was feeling the relief.

I took a deep breath myself and started to unload.

"John, I appreciate your candor. You were a big man on the court, and you're a big man now for coming out with it. We all get lost at times along our separate ways. I'm here today with you because I need a second chance. Slick needs a second chance, although I'm not going to discuss anything I say to the others. This is probably a good time for a course correction in life, for you, for me, the Back Court, the Coach, etc. I'm hoping, despite the distance, you can come up for a meeting, and hopefully I can get CB to be there."

"Now's the perfect time to give back. How about I start? I'll buy you dinner at Tommy's Pub on Colters Ave., as promised."

'You're on."

We headed for the back door. All the while we had been talking; the people that had been milling around inside the Ark were looking at us, but mostly at John. There goes that height again. However, no one stopped to inquire who he was. Still, it was awkward for us, and I got the feeling he was glad to leave the site of his past triumphs. Out in the lot he voiced the same conclusion I was thinking:

"I'll drive; I won't fit in your sardine can."

I laughed and hopped in the Escalade. He sped down the side street at 50 mph.

"John, you better ease off the pedal. These campus police can still be pretty nasty."

"I've always had a heavy foot. I did some stock car racing for kicks after I retired from the NBA."

I did read about that somewhere. He turned onto Colters Ave. and after passing under the train trestle, he slowed down when he approached the lawn where Tommy's once stood.

"A couple of blocks down on the left, John. They moved. There's a parking deck around the corner."

"You did tell me that, sorry."

When we got to the Pub, the same greeter was on duty.

"Are you Johnny Bird, from the Champ team?"

He didn't seem old enough to have seen John play, but he jabbered on for a few minutes about how great he was, etc. John was very gracious, and smiled sheepishly after each accolade. The greeter didn't remember me from the night before, or even look at me for that matter.

We sat down, and ate, drank, and talked for the better part of two hours. The topics ranged from car racing (he liked the sport mostly because he wouldn't get any speeding tickets, and the need for speed helped him drive slower among the populus); how he got into farming (his family were farmers in South Carolina for generations).

Eventually the conversation returned to basketball, and how best for him to get the second chance he needed to set his record straight. How he could be the prodigal son, and help Charlie Bennett in any way he could. I approached him with the idea of mentoring some of the young players. Not just those on the current roster, but those recent grads who were still “bouncing it” overseas. Skills, as well as life lessons could be offered. The internet would allow this.

“John, this basketball community at Sunnyside is going to be a family again.”

Our waitress came over with our check, which I grabbed, and she said,

“The manager took 50% off.”

We looked at the greeter, who waved to us. I guess if I was another player, I would have gotten away with just the tip.

He drove me back to the lot behind the Ark. He swallowed my hand in his again and said:

“John, I feel really good about what you and the Back Court are trying to do, and I feel really good about getting involved.”

“Have a safe trip home, and let’s never be more than a few clicks away.”

He sped off into the night, ignoring my reminder about the campus police. Maybe he was banking on the cop knowing who he was. I sat comfortably in my “sardine can,” and thought of the old ad Volkswagen ran with Wilt Chamberlain getting into a Beetle. They couldn’t do that with the Eos.

The car was facing the back door, so when I turned the lights on, I could see a smiling young John in the window. I flashed the lights a couple of times and rolled on home.

* * *

I slept like a baby. I got home tired but very content with the way things were going. Usually, it takes me a while to fall asleep. This morning I awoke with my arm stretched over the bed, which was unusual. I smiled, because I realized the last thing I remember, I was going to check to see what time Genna set the alarm, but I didn’t make it that far before the sandman intervened.

I didn't check my email last night, so I decided to do that first thing. Sidestepping the creaky floor boards, I crept up to the loft and the computer. I had mail from Quincy Wilson and Ken, but still no word from Charlie Bennett. Q said he was out in Los Angeles for a few weeks on vacation and business, but he left me an email and phone number to reach him. Slick must have put in a good word for me. Quincy was still the busiest one of the group, and being a coach or a scout in basketball is hellishly filled with travel miles. I didn't expect to hear from him so soon.

Ken was responding to my report about Slick (I pointedly emphasized to call him Reece in person). He said my back door play, or how we got this started, was a thing of beauty, and was I sure I didn't learn it from its master Pete Carill, the former great Princeton coach. He was very excited how things were going, and told me to check out the web site, which was ever improving and expanding. I noticed the reason he wanted me to check it out when I saw he added my bio and picture as the former player contact. The site was really shaping up; very clean, and succinctly describing everything we were about.

I guessed he would really be in the clouds when I told him John Bird was also on board, so I passed last night's rundown along to him.

I told Q via email how glad I was to hear from him so soon, and that I had heard from all of his teammates, except CB. Perhaps, I thought, Quincy would have better luck coaxing him to the keyboard. Since I understood he probably couldn't make it in person, I told him I would reach out by phone in a few days, to discuss what we were trying to do.

That was enough on the keyboard for now. I decided to call Byron Barrett later in the morning, to see where I could meet him. I headed downstairs and outside to collect the newspapers from the driveway. While coming back up the walk, I spied the answer to who was eating most of my plants and flower buds. This tiny rabbit, whose body was no longer than six inches, was nibbling away at the Japanese willow shrub I had just planted this season. I continued to walk very slowly towards him, and he didn't budge, all the while staring at me and nibbling contently. Approaching three feet before him, I slowly kneeled down before him while he continued to stare and munch away. He then showed me his modus to preparing his meal. He reached up and grabbed the stem of a branch, since the shrub's stems have an upward spray of growth, gnawed it off, and proceed to eat its leaves; all the while staring at me. I couldn't see the two little brass balls he was sitting on, but I was sure they were there.

I heard a faint whisper which formed words I could understand.

"You are one of my kindest creatures," the voice was saying to me. "All creatures can sense fear or friendship. The rabbit knows you will not harm him. The birds you feed let you stand next to the feeder because they know you're kind, and they can depend on you. I count people and creatures the same way, and they should be treated as such. All life lives and dies in many forms, forever. You seem to understand this. Your kindness will help me save many. I will remember your kindness to my flora and fauna in the garden while you must carry on down the path you are taking."

All the while this is being said, the rabbit continued to nibble and stare at me, as if to bear witness to my instructions. I slowly stood up straight, the rabbit loped past my feet, and into the dense foliage where I assumed he lived.

This little garden really was my piece of heaven.

I placed the papers on Genna's side of the table, and heard the sink water in the master bath. I glanced out the sliding door to the bird feeder over the deck rail to see several kinds of little chicks waiting to be fed. I gave them an extra helping today, as they hovered around until I was finished. The birds carried on at the feeder, reinforcing what Whoever made clear to me: they were people at one time. The finches are neat and respectful, the blue jays and crows are sloppy, disrespectful, and fight with everyone; and so on and on.

What a really good day so far.

* * *

"Hello, Byron. This is John from the Back Court. I hope I didn't catch you at a bad time."

"No, John, I'm sort of retired from youth counseling after twenty-five years. That was enough for me. I still do some moonlighting for a security agency, just to keep myself out of trouble, and stay out of my wife's hair; spaces in our togetherness; you know what I mean?"

"Sure do, I don't think too many marriages were designed for 24/7." (He must be a fan of Gibran's "*Prophet*," I thought).

"Amen. John, Slick was really upbeat after your talk with him. He sounded thirty years younger to me."

"Are you referring to Reece?"

Very loud laughter preceded Byron saying, "Don't make me drop the phone! He's a character."

"Anyway Byron, I'm glad he's enthusiastic. We all are. We see this as a "win win" for everyone. As a courtesy for your coming on board, I'd like to meet somewhere, and buy you dinner or lunch, whichever you prefer."

I was prepared to have him suggest a place close to his home. I didn't think I could play the Ark card again.

"John, Slick said he enjoyed seeing the old Ark again, maybe that would be a good place to meet first. From there, you can pick the restaurant or diner, it's up to you."

"I don't mind going back to the Ark," I said, "It's such a mystical place. John Bird said he could still hear the crowd, like holding a conch up to his ear. Then we could go to Raffael's, Delsomo, or Clintz. We have choices. We aim to please."

I didn't mention Tommy's Pub. Although I would like the chance at another one half check, I got a flashback of my piggish first date with Genna while dining with John.

“Raffael’s is my kind of place. I’m free tomorrow for lunch, how about you?”

“You’re on, Byron. Let’s meet at the Ark around 10:30?”

“See you then.”

I had searched the internet, so I knew some things about Byron’s bio. I knew he had retired from a career in youth counseling, and that he had his high school uniform retired, seeing pictures of both events. In a couple of articles, he was described as a homebody, and a devoted family man. He seemed to be living the cleanest life of all of them. Of any of his teammates, he seemed the least in need of a life path correction. I was looking forward to hear his take on things.

“John, did you have breakfast?”

Genna yelled from downstairs. I didn’t even hear her get up.

“No, I totally forgot. I guess I’m not that hungry.”

At the sentence end, I heard her coffee grinder blast off. For the next thirty seconds, if all the windows were open, we could wake up all the neighbors. Fortunately, they’re all probably up anyway. I decided to go to the kitchen to have a cup of green tea and a banana. Antioxidants and potassium; I felt healthier already.

Genna really likes basketball, but the Back Court doings are stretching it a bit for her. I decided to risk her humoring me at the breakfast table.

“The club is really exciting this year. Ken’s doing a great job, and we’re getting a great response so far reaching out to former players.”

“Ummmm.” I failed to get her nose out of the newspaper, so I changed the subject.

“Your left breast is hanging out of your pajama top, thank you very much.”

“Ummm….what did you say?”

"Never mind. Any news that's fit to squint?"

"Samo."

Jean Michel Basquiat, rest in peace.

Since the conversation wasn't going anywhere, I finished my tea and banana, and added:

"Enjoy the rest of your cereal."

She eats this supposedly very healthy gruel which I know tastes like minced cardboard, and I have a hard time watching her eat it.

"I'm finally going for my walk today. See you in a bit."

I forgot my walk. I forgot my breakfast. I was having my best day in awhile regardless.

Chapter Fourteen

I was beginning to wonder if the security guard at the Ark may start to suspect me and my associates of casing the place, with the intent to do harm. He may have watched us scanning the inside from rafter to court, any number of times in the past few weeks. John the terrorist, that's me. While I was waiting for Byron, I put the facts straight in my head, so if confronted, I wouldn't seem haltingly suspicious. I wasn't there long when a late model Caddy de Ville pulled up near the door, and out steps Byron. These big guys need big cars. As soon as he saw me standing there, he got the "I know this guy" look on his face.

"Hi Byron, do you remember me?"

"Yes I do. It was a few years back at the SAC, right?"

"Yes, you were with Harry Hoppe. Do you remember what I said to you both?"

"I sure do. I see Harry probably more than anyone on the team, and you've come up in conversation a few times. That story you told meant a lot to us both."

'Well, I really meant it. I don't know where I'd be today if I didn't flip THAT dial at THAT moment."

I could see he was anxious to get inside the Ark.

"When was the last time you were here?"

"Oh, gosh, about fifteen years ago. I happened to be driving near the campus on an errand, and something made me pull in the lot, for old time's sake. It was at night, and I thought the place would be locked up. I came to this very door, and I thought I heard a "click" as I approached it. Nah, I thought, but it was open, just some night lights inside for me not to trip on anything. I also remember there was a cool draft inside; sort of gave me the creeps. I just looked around real quick and went back outside. I had goose bumps, and I haven't been back since."

His story began to give ME goose bumps; it was eerily similar to the way I wound up at the Ark. Maybe Byron was the first one to get the call to soothe these souls before I was chosen. Who knows what may have happened if he stayed inside a while longer before getting the creeps, then fleeing. Slick may have tapped him on the shoulder instead of me. We were about to find out if he would make the same connection as I did.

"Let's see whose inside now, I wouldn't be surprised if this place did have ghosts," I said cheekily, which he didn't pick up on.

In addition to the usual suspects milling around inside, folding chairs were being set up for some kind of entertainment that evening.

"I see this old place is still a multi-use venue," Byron commented on the activity.

"It sure is," I followed, noting that he was unaware of the Sunny - Megamont game going on amidst the other hoopla. "Do you sense a presence as Johnny Bird did; can you hear any crowd noise?"

"Not any crowd noise, but faint squeaks, like sneakers make on the court. Almost the same sound during the scrimmages we used to have here. In that sense, it's almost like old times. I've had dreams occasionally where I'm still playing parts of the Megamont game over in my head. These dreams are very vivid, like almost real. When I wake up, I have to pinch myself."

I smiled. It seems Byron was almost privy to what I was witness to, but not quite. As I'm talking to him, I'm trying not to look at the game in progress, as Slick is hot dogging, trying to get my attention; and the 1971 Byron is on the sideline watching us talk.

"When I first came back to this place," I told him, "I had a weird feeling just looking at the places I used to sit and watch games. If you actually played, it must be a much stronger memory."

An even weirder feeling when Slick tapped me on the shoulder, I thought.

"Byron, if you've seen enough, we can go to Raffael's, and beat the lunch crowd."

He agreed, "At least this visit, I didn't get goose bumps." We left by the back door. He took another look at my little Eos, and motioned me to get in his Caddy.

"So Byron, what made you decide to contact me and the Back Court at this time?"

"Well, I wasn't going to, until I heard from Slick. Not responding had nothing to do with the slight about the team's fortieth anniversary. It doesn't bother me as much as the other guys. I'm at peace with just about everything. I feel blessed to have played basketball as long as I did. I feel I made a difference in my working life; I was able to turn around more than a few kids that were going down the wrong path. There's so much love that I give and get between my wife and four kids. I'm basically a homebody who feels he's been given enough to work with and be happy about. Slick convinced me that this should be about Charlie Bennett. He was our hero then, and he needs our help now. He's kind of despondent about everything."

"I gathered that from my conversations so far. I still haven't heard from him; he's the last one I'm waiting on."

We lucked out with a parking spot two doors down from Raffael's. I have the worst luck finding a good parking space. Had I driven, we'd be at the parking deck two blocks, instead of two spaces, away. Getting the good space was a good sign we beat the crowd. We walked up to the greeting station, and noticed all eyes of the staff and the few patrons were on 6' 7" Byron. I motioned toward a back table out of traffic, which the greeter then seated us at.

I knew there was something else I liked about Byron when he ordered a Bass pint.

"Two, please," I added.

"How are we going to get CB to come on board? This Champ slight must bother him the most. Any ideas?"

"Charlie's always been a tough nut to crack, especially in recent years. I think it bothers him and has made him more withdrawn, that his success has receded behind the rest of us. The past few years have been more messages, and less returned calls from CB. I'll keep calling him, we all will, but he's got to pick up."

"I would appreciate the rest of you continuing to reach out to him. When you do get through, tell him we want him to help us finish what he started."

Byron looked at me and understood the angle of my appeal.

We continued talking, but off topic about our families. He got married a little later than usual, so his children were in their teens, and his son is starting to show some promise on the court.

"I hope he makes it to Sunnyside," I said, to which he smiled hopefully.

He worked on his hanger steak while I did the same on my grilled shrimp salad, and we washed them down with another round of Bass.

I paid the tab when we finished, and we walked out of a very crowded restaurant. A few recognized Byron, just enough to say "hi" without engaging in conversation. I began hoping Byron would be the one to reach Charlie. I had a feeling his inner calm and peace would provide the needed tug on Charlie's psyche. Once he got him to make the call to me, I knew I would close the sale. If he couldn't do it, I was betting on motor mouth Slick as the next best chance.

He observed the speed limit on the way back to the Ark lot; he wasn't a hot foot like Mr. Bird. Byron had the most even keeled personality I'd seen in a while. He didn't need inspiration or encouragement. He had the same contented look on his face while leaving as arriving.

"BB, thanks for your efforts with CB (as if to thank him in advance). I've met him a couple of times, but he may not remember me. He stands a better chance of listening to his teammates at this point than to me. Here's hoping."

He gave me the same broad smile as before, and a thumbs up as he pulled out of the lot; not noticing his younger self at the door window.

* * *

"Ken," I emailed, "I had another really good talk with Byron Barrett. He and his teammates are making a concerted effort to get Charlie Bennett off the fence. If we're able to convince him, the credibility of our effort will increase tenfold," which was true, without mentioning again that it was the right thing to do.

I decided to call the number Quincy Wilson gave me; I just might get lucky, or continue to be lucky, as things were going well with this endeavor.

A very girlish, breathy female voice answered the phone, almost like Jackie Kennedy, but younger.

"Mr. Wilson's office."

I thought he gave me his cell phone number.

"Mr. Wilson is expecting my call. When do you think he can return it?"

"He should be back later this afternoon. I'll tell him you called."

This could be telephone tag in the making. In the meantime, I'll give Harry Hoppe a call. Better luck this time.

"This is Harry."

"Harry, this is John from the Back Court." I just met with Byron, and he remembered when I met the both of you at the SAC a few years ago."

"That was you? John that was one of the best stories a fan ever told me."

"Does that include true stories as well as bullshit?" I asked.

"One of the best of any kind," he laughed heartily.

I did mention earlier that Hal was a car dealer, but was also a very savvy investor which made me slip in the question:

"Got any tips?"

"I don't go to the racetrack."

It was my turn to chuckle, but I got the impression he didn't offer any free advice on the market.

"Harry, I've gotten very good responses from your teammates, except Charlie, who I haven't heard from yet."

Let's get that up front, I thought, to give it main topic status.

"I hope you'll join in. We want to at least approach the excitement your Champ team had. You can share in the fun, and show us how it's done."

A poet and I didn't know it. I hoped I didn't come off sounding like a huckster.

"Byron's a really fine gentleman, at peace with himself," I quickly added this more reasonable assessment.

"That he is. I probably spent more time with him than any of the others, when he wants to get out of the house, which isn't that often. The guy is a real homebody. CB is also in the area, but he has withdrawn in recent years. It's got us worried, as a matter of fact. I guess you've talked to enough of us to know we owe him, and want to bring the old Charlie back."

"You're right. You all have different reasons, but the common thread is to help Charlie. Do you have a particular reason of your own?"

He fielded my curveball nicely, and gave a sigh before he began.

"The year after the Champ season, I caught the Johnny Bird disease. I don't know if he admitted it to you, but he became very selfish his sophomore year onward."

I didn't nod or answer, wanting to keep each conversation confidential.

"I said to myself, 'You know what?' I'm going to pad my stats too. We're both going to the NBA, not just him. I was the upper classman; I should be getting the first touch before him."

What he meant was the first to touch the ball in an offensive set can decide to shoot the ball first.

"I still love him like a younger brother, but after the magic year, we were feeding on instead of off each other, and at times it got ugly in the locker room. We both let the team down, but I blame myself for going along with it. I've had enough success in the rest of my life, and I have given back to the school and my community, but that selfishness back then has gnawed at me over the years. I wish I had a second chance do over."

"Since you can't have that, giving back to someone near and dear to you is a close second, correct?"

"John, that's the way I see it."

"As I've asked the others, keep on Charlie to join us. You know I have a stake in this also, remember my story."

"Harry," I continued, "Did any of the others tell you about meeting at the Ark?"

"Slick did. That place must be like some sort of 'soul center' if you know what I mean. He said the place has good vibes."

Does it ever, more than you know, Harry, and he is describing it with the lingo of the 70s.

"Harry, like I told the others, we in the club appreciate your willingness to help out, so I'd like to buy you lunch, dinner, or a couple of rounds whenever is convenient for you."

"John, I've been a little busy with business tanking lately, but I'll take a rain check."

"OK. I'll send you an email from time to time. Maybe pot luck someday soon we'll be able to work it."

"Sounds good, I talk to you soon."

Click.

I wasn't placing any bets that Quincy Wilson would call me later, but hope doesn't require a wager.

Chapter Fifteen

As I said, "Quick" Quincy Wilson was the spark plug, or the point guard on the court. However, he was also the spark plug off the court, and his partying antics were legendary. Quite a few coeds would tell you he was quick alright. "Work hard, play hard," for Quincy was, "play hard, play hard." He was tamed over time, and learned to burn only one end of the candle.

I did mention he was the only one on the Champ team to earn a championship ring in the Pros. He did it as a solid backup player, after bouncing around the league, and landing on the right team at the right time. After his playing days, his knowledge of the game, and personable nature endeared him to the right connections in the coaching fraternity to move up that ladder, also. Ultimately, he landed on the bench next to one of, if not the best, coaches ever to draw an "x" or an "o" in a huddle. Quincy mined his head for all those golden nuggets of coaching wisdom, including the intricate variations of the back door play that I'm sure you know by now is my favorite.

"You've got mail," crackled through my speakers.

It was a nice surprise to hear from Kyle Keiderling. Kyle's my old seat mate at the SAC. A few years ago he retired out West, but he's still avid with his concerns for the Sunny program. He's a writer who does carefully researched books about college basketball; the one about Hank Gathers, *Heart of a Lion,* comes to mind. Hank was the Loyola Marymount player who collapsed and died on the court in the early 1990's.

I decided to give him a call.

"Hello," I said, "this is your delinquent friend. Hope all is well. Why don't you come east, and join the hurricane party?"

We were expecting a major storm by the weekend.

I gave him a rundown of the Back Court renaissance which he thought was long overdue, but he also saw it from a different, but equally attractive viewpoint.

"John, I can't tell you how many times in my research, former players who got into coaching, sent their best players to their alma mater."

It made sense to me.

He asked me to save him a few tickets for the upcoming season, which I always do. He comes east a lot doing book tours.

"I'll call you as soon as the schedule comes out," I said.

Kyle turned out to be the lucky charm of the day. I no sooner clicked off his call when I got an incoming from California.

"Hi, is this John?"

"That's me, is this quick Quincy? You did get back to me pretty quickly. How's your first step these days?"

The "first step" for a basketball player usually decides his advantage for a move to the basket, or to an area for an open shot; quickness being the key. As a player ages, that quickness is usually the first thing to go.

"Not like it used to be, John," he said with a chuckle. "When I heard from Reece, he was wound up like a top. What the hell did you say to him?"

"Reece? Who's Reece?" I said sarcastically, "Oh, you mean Slick?"

Quincy laughed a little harder at this remark, and I added:

"I just want you to know Q, your other teammates are still inclined to call him 'Slick', just not to his face. It's almost a private joke, but I'll never tell."

"Quincy, Slick and I had a really good talk. We spoke about the basketball program moving forward, not looking backward. We talked about second chances. The vast majority of people, if they had a do over, would change something about their life they've come to regret. I'm one of those people, and so is Slick. So are John and Harry. I'd have to say Byron is an exception. He has other reasons to get involved, but he is still fully committed to helping. What are your thoughts about our appeal, Q?"

"John, I think it's time for me to start giving back to Sunnyside. During my playing days in the Pros, and during my coaching tenures, I didn't have much time, but I didn't look to make any time either. Now, with my coaching career winding down, it's the time to make up. It's another chance for me to make an impact on a kid or two, so they have the chance I had."

Quincy was in the majority; the second chancers who wanted to make good. I had to tell him my behind-the-scenes efforts a short while ago.

"Quincy, I have to tell you this story which happened during the last coaching search, before we hired Manny Wheaton. I made the argument to the AD the time might be right to approach you about the head coaching job at your alma mater. I told him you had your ring from a Pro championship. Possibly, I told him, you might be ready to ease up, and give something back to your school. Soon after I emailed him, I started hearing rumors that he approached you about the job. Did he?"

"Yes he did, John. I gave it a hard look, and realized I couldn't do it. When I was an assistant coach in the college ranks, I hated recruiting. You have to love recruiting players in college to be successful at that level."

"I thought that was your take on recruiting, so I argued that your assistants would do the recruiting, and you would just close the sale in the living room with the parents and the player."

"I wish it worked that way, John. It's really about long term relationships. You have to start with these kids when they're in 7th grade.

Anyway, it did get me thinking in due time I should contribute something to the program."

"So, schedule permitting, you could make it to a couple of Back Court meetings?" I said when I saw this opening.

"That's my plan, John, and I'm looking to increase my involvement in future years."

"Quincy. I have one other question. Have you ever been back inside the Ark since your playing days?"

"Almost. About ten years ago, when I was still coaching in the area, the thought just popped into my head to drop in. It was early evening, and I was actually heading over there. However, I got a call from an assistant coach about a pressing basketball matter, so that put the kibosh on my visit. It was very strange how the idea just appeared out of the blue. It was like I started to enter a magnetic field, and was gradually being drawn there. That was the only time I got the urge to go there."

"Quincy, I can tell you I've met a couple of your teammates there, and they all agree it's a magical place still. You should meet me there someday soon, if possible. When will you be near the Philly?"

"Maybe the day of a Back Court meeting that I can attend, I'll stop over. I'll let you know."

I thought he was about to hang up, when I heard a slight sigh on his end.

"There is another reason I'd like to get involved. It's about Charlie Bennett. They honored him at half time about four years ago; the rest of the team was there, and he looked like hell. We were all appalled. He was doing a little better after that boost, but he's slid backwards again. I guess you've figured out that part. We're in this for Charlie."

"Yes, I have. Quincy, I've asked your teammates, and now I'm asking you, keep trying to have him make the call. He's the only one I haven't heard from."

"I will."

"Thanks again for your renewed interest and good luck with CB."

He hung up sounding sincerely interested.

I had more good news for Ken Blarney.

* * *

The next day I was surfing the web after I sent an email to Ken about the Quincy conversation. I was searching various databases about the recruiting wars of different school basketball programs in the area. After a short while the exercise became mind numbing, and I started mulling the recent conversations I had with my modern day "ghosts." Just as I was starting to pat myself on the back a bit too much, I got an Instant Message from Ken:

"John, this is short notice, but the Back Court board members are meeting in two days at Williams Hall, on the third floor, at 6:30 P.M. Can you make it? There are going to be some people from the basketball office there with the blessing of Manny Wheaton, and I want you to give them a recap so far about your meetings. I think they'll be surprised with our progress on that front, and we'll be able to dispel the doubts Coach Wheaton had with the idea."

"See you there."

Nothing out of the ordinary happened during the next two days that you need to know about. There was still no word from Charlie Bennett despite five guys who really cared trying to pry him loose from whatever was holding him back.

I cruised up Route 20 around a quarter to six and snickered at the log jam of cars heading the other way. I've had a few other meetings at Williams Hall for other matters, and always enjoyed the design of the building inside and out. It's located in the oldest and prettiest part of the College. I think the Castellini Chapel on the campus was designed by Henry Hardenbergh, a contemporary of my guy Frank Lloyd Wright whom Wright had a modicum of respect for. What I just said was actually a lot, because Wright had little or no respect for anyone in his field during his career. Hardenberg's other designs were the Dakota Apartments, the Waldorf Astoria and Plaza hotels. Wright's respect was demonstrated by his extended stay at the Plaza while overseeing the Guggenheim's construction, his masterpiece museum in New York City.

Van Dyke Taylor was the designer of Williams Hall, a minor figure in the architecture of his day, however a favorite of mine for his work on our meeting spot.

Passing through the gates into that area of the college is like returning to the late nineteenth century when those campus buildings were built. If you don't let your eyes wander beyond the block of the Campus, this feeling is real. Being my customary fifteen minutes early, I got a good space to minimize the soaking rain promised after the meeting adjourned.

Ken was the only one in the room when I trudged up to the third floor, and he flashed a broad smile when he saw me. He slid a copy of the agenda across the table, and in his animated way started rattling off the key points as if everyone was already there.

"Ken, I think you should wait for the others."

He laughed, and said, "Sorry, this is a very exciting time for me. We in the club haven't had this much traction in years."

"Well," I added, "Let's make it worth the wait."

After another fifteen minutes, everyone else sauntered into the meeting room, and Ken revved up his spiel again regarding the various ways the club was going to raise money for the program. He went on at length about membership, auctions, apparel sales, 50/50 ticket chances; he was channeling PT Barnum like no other.

There were four young guys from the basketball office who were taking all of this in very enthusiastically. It was nice to see their encouragement and willingness to help, instead of a "you can't do that" refrain that we were all too used to hearing.

Ken gradually came to my topic of interest regarding former players, and what we should be doing for and with them.

"John. Why don't you recap what we've heard so far from the alums?"

I launched into the list of former players I'd heard from, starting from the most current, recent grads, and worked my way back into Sunnyside basketball history. I dwelled on the players who were on teams that made it to "The Dance," the NCAA tournament. I ended my recaps, of course, with the Champ team. I gave them all the head's up on Slick's name change to Reece. I told them John Bird's hot foot hadn't cooled off. I produced some chuckles with these, and other anecdotes about Harry, Byron, and Quincy. Pausing to let the smirking subside, I dosed them with reality:

"Fellas, I've heard from these guys for various personal reasons, but the common one is they're all worried about Charlie Bennett. He's the only one of the group I haven't heard from. They all tell me he's in a bad way. Life's been creeping up on him. This recession has hit him hard. He lost his job, and has had to take a series of menial ones to make ends meet. I know there are a lot of Sunny grads enduring similar hardships, but this guy is special to us, we owe him big time."

I adjusted my gaze to the four horsemen of the basketball office:

"Charlie Bennett put us on the map forty years ago. Without him, we don't get to the Champ game that year. Most of the teams that were our doormats in 1971, are at the Dance almost every year, and we're not even close to that. The AD and the Program at the time squandered his accomplishment."

I could see I was making a few people uncomfortable, so I backed off a little.

"Look, all I want to say at this time is our former athletes deserve better. They bring a lot more to the school than the scholarship they receive. I'm not thinking of money. They show us how to work hard; 'to fill the unforgiving minute with 60 seconds worth of distance run'." Thank you, Kipling.

"Guys, these players deserve more respect. Let's bring them on the crest of the wave we're all starting to catch."

I suspected if everyone around the table had their druthers, we would be going back to the Dance this year. The level of enthusiasm was to that boiling point; although no one was coming right out with it, not wanting to seem unrealistically foolish this time next year, if we didn't make it. However, I decided to be the first one to spill my beans.

"I've talked to some of the current players, and the new recruits, and they're all thinking 'Dance' this year, and why not? Let's think as Big as they are."

A few around the table smiled sheepishly without conviction. Ken in particular, for all his enthusiasm, always has a tempered reserve, which I find incongruous. No one else, although secretly hoping I was right, was willing to put his tit in the ringer like I did. Without a second thought, I turned to the four horsemen and said:

"You guys tell Coach Wheaton that I publicly, and they privately, think he can do it this year." I added a smile to the delivery.

Ken gave me a little eye roll, and that "there he goes again" look.

The meeting was over.

Chapter Sixteen

Two days later, Ken called me, a rarity from his customary emails.

"Coach Wheaton wants to have a combination pep rally, player appreciation night. It would be honoring the teams that have made it to the Dance. He wants to hold it not at the SAC, but at the Ark. The event would be held sometime before the start of the Coastal East schedule, around mid December, before the holidays. Admission would be charged, probably around thirty bucks, or free if you were a Back Court member. This would probably help our membership."

"Why don't we charge twenty bucks, or if they join the club for fifty, they get a twenty dollar tee shirt for free? I guess coach is on board with the former player initiative?"

"Is he ever! I mean big time. He now sees this as an opportunity to make a statement to the NCAA; like the school is taking care of its ex-players, while you, the NCAA are not. He wants to make them look bad, but in a nice way, by example. He thinks down the road, it will force them to have some kind of support program network."

This was all music to my ears, and I couldn't have hoped for a better outcome for my efforts. The event was being planned for about three months in advance, so we had time to do our homework. I thought Ken must be salivating on the other end of the phone.

"Ken, this is fabulous, the more I think about it. There's lots of ways we can do it, but one thing has to happen between now and then: Charlie

Bennett has to agree to be there. Without him, it'll be like having a wedding without the groom, don't you agree?"

"I hear you. What else can we do to affect that happening?"

"I'll try to think of something, but for now his teammates are all working on him. I think they're our best shot. I'm still thinking that they, and maybe Manny picking up the phone, will get the job done."

"John, isn't it nice to see some cooperation?"

"Ken, it's more like cooperation with a back flip thrown in. When is the next club function?"

"Coach is going to have us come to a practice in early October; just the club."

"That's neat, just a couple of weeks away. They should have his defense down pat by then."

We both laughed in unison, but it wasn't really a laughing matter. Although the outcome of a contest is determined by the most points, defense wins games. With so many young freshmen on the roster, getting them to grasp Coach Wheaton's intricate defensive schemes was asking a lot. Hopefully, enough of them were quick studies. That would be the only way we were going dancing this year.

"John, let's keep in touch?"

"Bye for now."

I sat in silence for more than a few moments, letting what was going to happen in about three months sink in. I began to construct a model in my head of the event. Screaming fans egged beyond a fever pitch. An auctioneer hustling bids on various keepsakes. Barkers soliciting 50/50 chance raffles while during this carnival Sunnyside and Megamont are playing for the umpteenth time; blurring the real life proceedings enough to make my head explode. Just as I was getting a headache just from anticipation of all this, a sudden calm came over me. There were no voices or cooling sea breezes, just a relaxing of all the muscles in my body, sending a "be all right" message with a slow exhale.

* * *

Friday morning about a week later was not very kind to me. The night before I had my usual twilight episode, but instead of sleeping it off, I tossed all night. Earlier in the week we had a major storm pass us which caused a lot of damage to the area, but just knocked the power out for almost two days at our house. I felt bad for my elderly parents because they drove an hour and a half to be with us, and their house never lost power. I was guessing the stress had upset my biorhythms; a possible explanation why I had that twilight feeling this morning. Having this feeling in the morning felt like I was still between a dream and a nightmare.

When I don't wake up one hundred percent, I force myself to continue my routine, and work through the discomfort; "tough it out," so to speak. So this morning, the gargling, the tall glass of water, and the brisk heel and toe through the neighborhood did do the trick. The shower routine helped even more, and I felt fully awake again. I made another mental note to see my doctor if this persists.

With all that was going on the past few weeks, I was curious about the activity at the Ark. That big old whale of a building which, compared to its history, was on life support regarding activity level. However, in a few months it would feel the glory days again. After breakfast and perusing the paper with Genna, I would head there.

"I have to go to the Ark to speak to someone about the event the club is having there soon." I checked off another half fib on my account.

"I have an appointment with the chiropractor."

Genna has a back with a mind of its own. Sometimes if she turns left, her back goes right. Regular maintenance seems to keep it in check, and this was one of those visits.

"Genna, I ought to be home by early afternoon. We can scheme the rest of the day then."

"You're on your own. After the chiro, I need some toiletries, and I have to get your mother a birthday present."

"OK." I began thinking of stretching this afternoon into a hanger steak dinner, and a Bass pint at Raffael's.

I arrived at the Ark lot two and a half hours later, a trip that normally takes a half hour to forty- five minutes. After a major storm, the banks of the Nemacole River, on which the Sunnyside College town sits, just disappears. There's the river, then the city streets. I ended up taking a long, circuitous route to bypass the flooding. The main campus is on higher ground, but to get there from the south after a storm, you need a boat.

I was pretty exhausted from taking this scenic route, and just when I turned the car off, the voice said:

"Find him."

I sat there for a few moments trying to figure out who "him" was. I guessed going inside, I would find out.

The fall semester was in full swing on the campus, and the Ark had a slightly quickened pulse than in the summer, but not like the old days. The chairs were still straddling the court like a seated battalion of soldiers; remnants of this year's orientation most likely. They were facing a stage that workmen and roadies were playing with sound equipment and lighting. Come to think of it, the school staged a concert a few weeks after we checked in freshman year. I bet they follow a similar script year in and year out. Boring, but easier, I guess.

Not long after this observation, I noticed the Megamont team, and five Sunnyside players shooting baskets at either end of the court, without much purpose or resolve. Slick nodded in my direction, without bothering his customary smile, and walked my way. That's when it hit me.

"Slick, where's Charlie?"

"We can't find him. He's got us sick. He's been on a roller coaster; up one day, down the next. This is the first time he's disappeared though. The Megamont team doesn't want to play us without him. We've looked everywhere."

"Everywhere?" I asked, "Where the hell could he go?" I realized the ridiculousness of what I just said, judging by the size of the Universe.

"Do you still think he's in the building, or could he be somewhere else in the Cosmos?" I pushed further.

"We all sense his presence in the building, but we can't find him. We've looked every …"

"Except one place." I finished his sentence. "I'll be right back."

I walked briskly towards the door leading to the swimming pool in the basement under the court. Picking up speed, I shuffled down the stairs, and almost stepped in the disinfectant tray outside the pool room door. It looked like the swimming coach was having time trials for team members to see who worked the hardest over the summer. All lanes were splashing, whistles were blowing, and hangers on were cheering the men-fish in the water.

The corner of my eye caught Charlie Bennett sitting in the farthest seat from the pool. His hands gripped his elbows tightly, and he was shaking to the point I thought I had blurred vision. I glanced around to see if I was being looked at suspiciously. Slowly, to look like I belonged, I made my way up the bleachers and sat next to CB. No one else was sitting close by, but I cautiously whispered out of the corner of my mouth:

"Charlie, what the hell are you doing here? The guys are sick to death worrying about you."

"It's no use, John. I'm just wasting everybody's time. I know the other guys are here for me, but we've wasted the better part of forty years. I'm the reason they're not at peace. I want to just go jump in that pool and melt away. I have a feeling inside that I don't ever amount to anything.

The least I can do is make the other guys stop worrying. If I'm not around here, they can all go home; wherever that is."

'But try as you may, you can't just run down there and jump in that pool, can you?"

"No, I can't. I want to, but it's like two negative sides of a magnet."

"Charlie, you can't put an end to this because you're not done yet. Did you ever have a coach who rode you like a jockey, until you were ready to drop? He did that because he didn't want to see you fail. There's Somebody out there who makes you keep trying. As long as you still try, you haven't failed. You are closer than you think to finishing what you started, and you're the only one who can lead the cavalry."

He looked a little puzzled by this imagery, but he seemed to understand the part about the coach who pushed him.

"Now I'd like you to go back out the way you came in before all this chlorine makes me throw up."

He sheepishly walked down the side isle furthest from the pool and out the door. I think he was embarrassed by what he thought of doing, but his tremors relaxed as soon as he left the pool room. As he stepped through the door (before I opened it for myself) and stepped onto the court, he was greeted by shakes and hugs, smacks upside his head, and even a few smiles from the stoic Mega players.

CB gave me one more glance, and I took that opportunity to say:

"Now go drop forty on these guys!"

I didn't need to watch any of the game. I headed straight for the back door, the Eos, the hanger steak, and TWO pints of Bass at Raffael's.

Chapter Seventeen

The next week was much better. The effects of the storm were being corrected. The roads, trees, and other damage were cleaned like they never happened, at least in our neck of the woods; not so for much of the Northeast, however.

The day finally arrived for the coach's open practice for the Back Court members. I hopped in the Eos, and was glad Route 20 was passable again.

I was sitting in the bleachers at the SAC; having arrived much earlier than my usual fifteen minutes. For some reason, I'm at the SAC one minute after the doors open. Hardly anyone was there yet, just a few other event staff members, me, and a few thoughts. My mind wandered back to what Charlie said last week, about having a feeling that he wasn't going to amount to anything later in life. I found it sad that just because he wasn't long in years of accomplishments, he felt they didn't add up to him. His were deeds of some, and dreams of most others. I was hoping that last pep talk would be enough to pull him through. He didn't know what was about to happen in a couple of months, but I did.

Ken's tap on my shoulder ended the daydream. I also noticed a steady stream of BC members had filtered into the SAC; none of them disturbing my thought.

"Coach wants to talk to the both of us after the meeting, probably about the Ark event. He's really done a 180, it's almost like he went to school here."

We both laughed with satisfaction over this.

"How has the team looked so far? You've seen them practice before this, right?"

"You'll see soon enough. I think you may be right about our prospects this year, barring any serious injuries."

The players started to drift onto the court. Ken and I got some nods of hello from those who played in the summer league. After that, it was all business. Warm-ups and stretching were supervised by various trainers. Forward and lateral defensive postures created the appearance of giant crabs taking over the court. Watching this action reminded me a few years back when the team that had just won the Championship came to the SAC. The warm up drills they executed were as precise as a drum and bugle corps: a thing of beauty. We're not, but are getting there.

Manny Wheaton and the rest of his staff took to the court, a whistle in his mouth. A sharp chirp got the players attention, and started a string of expletives that peppered emphasis to all he was teaching.

Ken was right. These guys have no trouble putting the ball in the hole, and they were really grasping the defensive alignments. On defense, most of the freshmen had a good sense of when to gamble, and when not to. It all said one thing to me: the talent level was way up. This wasn't a game yet, of course, but Manny seemed pleased with what they'd gotten under their belts so far; and the praises were outweighing the butt kicks. If a player made a bad or stupid mistake, he had to take off and run up the aisle to the nose bleed seats, and that didn't happen too often during this practice.

The wonderment I have about a good coach is their ability to watch ten players at once. Most fans, especially the casual ones, just watch the ball. A good coach watches everything else but. I remember watching some practice footage of Manny Wheaton demonstrating this gift, before he was hired. He chirped his whistle to stop the practice, and nearly ripped the head off a player who was furthest from the ball, who was not giving it his all.

"Young man, don't cheat on my court," he barked at the player, before sending him stair stepping up the aisle to the rafters.

That closed the sale for me wanting him to come to Sunny.

The practice ended with the players doing back and forth sprints, or "suicides" for about ten minutes. Manny Wheaton berated the slower players almost to tears, but everyone knew they needed enduring legs for forty plus minutes a game to be successful.

After the last dripping player left the court, and some small talk to the rest of the club before they also left, Coach Wheaton gave Ken and I a hand and head motion for us to come with him. The three of us sat down in a quiet corner of the gym.

I offered first, "Coach, I think you're going to have a couple of signature wins this year that aren't going to depend on a three point play in the final second, or any kind of luck like that."

"John, that wasn't luck. I drew up that play."

The three of us laughed in unison; this was a much better opening remark than the "f**k you" comment when we first met. I decided to continue to lead the conversation.

"Coach, we've gotten a good response so far from the alums. It's early. There will be more to come, we're sure. We're really excited about the Ark event to kick off the Coastal East schedule, are you?"

"John, I think it can be a really good event, but I'm concerned about the format and content. That's why you're both here."

I turned to the person on my left, and said:

"Ken?"

He launched into his P.T. Barnum routine without missing a beat. I knew when I opened first, he would be winding himself like a top. I just stood back and watched Disney animation personified launch into the promotions, auctions, raffles, etc, ending with a select group of former players saying a few words each, to keep the fever high at the Ark. Ken seemed exhausted at the end of his rant, like a top starting to teeter, but he sold the goods.

"Ken and John, you guys run with it; I'm fully behind it."

Ken looked at me to bring up the missing ingredient for the Ark rally.

"Coach, there's something we may have to ask you to do for us. Although the response to the letter that went out has been very encouraging, we still haven't heard from Charlie Bennett. As you must know by now (I was hoping), he was the centerpiece of the first and last team that went to the Champ. All of his teammates admit they wouldn't have gotten there without CB. There's still time, but if we don't hear from him soon, would you make a call for us? It'll be a much better event if he is there. He's the centerpiece of the history of this program."

From the expression on his face, I could see the coach took this request as a curveball, which I couldn't see why. However, after a few more seconds, he said:

"Sure."

He abruptly got up and shook both our hands vigorously, said good bye, and loped toward the locker room. He had to give his salt and pepper assessment of the workout to the players after they showered, and before they headed off to class, students again.

"Way to go Phineas!" the 'P' in Barnum, my new nickname for Ken, which might stick. "What's the next step?"

"Let's keep in touch with the teammates, and hope they can get to him."

"Read anything into the coach's reluctance?"

"Not really, maybe he doesn't like talking, or in this case groveling, to someone he doesn't know from Adam."

"Did you ever consider a career in sales?"

"Nah, I couldn't do this day in day out. I'll stick to mixing chemicals for the body."

We walked to our cars in the SAC lot, and sped off in different directions.

Another good day in a good week.

Chapter Eighteen

As I've gotten older, I'm not at all convinced that time is a constant. I know I could stare at the second hand on my watch as it paces the same rate ahead of history. It just seems that I've gotten older faster than when I was younger. I'm not talking about the physical nature of aging, but the events in my life. They just seem to approach faster and are gone.

So it was with the upcoming basketball season. From that meeting after the practice, until the opening exhibition game of the season went by in a blur. I kept busy. I tried to answer most of the questionnaires that the alums sent back, as well as keeping in touch with the '71 teammates. The only thing that made time go a little slower was still not hearing from CB. They all relayed his same response to them; he'd think about it, and they all took this as a brush off. I really hoped they would ultimately be successful, because I was hesitant to ask Coach Wheaton to make that call. I knew he would, but he wouldn't want to.

Regardless, that first exhibition game was a tour de force, for the young team and especially Manny Wheaton. The game itself is a first come, first serve regarding your choice of seats. Genna and I got there as soon as the doors opened to get front row seats behind the Sunny bench, in order to hear Manny's "color" commentary. He did not disappoint. I had reminded Genna to just snicker, and not laugh loudly at his curse filled cajoles. She did manage to get through the game without bursting her gut. This type of game is for the squad of players, the old and the new, to mesh their timing and get used to a real game. They won handily, but as usual, Manny wanted more.

We were leaving our seats when I heard:

"Hey John."

The voice was familiar, and could only come from one person.

"Reece, it's good to see you. Remember Genna?"

His flashy smile was broader than usual.

"I'll let you guys talk. I have to go to the lady's room," Genna said as she quick stepped up the aisle.

"Is there good news behind those pearly whites?" I asked.

"He's coming."

"You mean Charlie, I hope?"

"Yup. He called me yesterday, sounding like the Charlie of forty years ago."

"I'm just curious. Did he say what changed his mind? It sounds like you were talking to a different person."

"It gets a little bizarre here. He said he had a revelation, a dream that he was talking to his younger self, dressed in his old playing uniform for Sunny. The younger Charlie kept saying to him 'finish what you started, finish what you started ….' CB said he woke up feeling a new desire to make a difference; once again through basketball. He said he feels like a new person. The old aches, pains, and sports injuries don't hurt as much. He's looking at the future again, not at the past."

I was fumbling with my thoughts upon hearing this, but I did manage to ask,

"Do you think he would say a few words at the rally?"

"John, I took the liberty to ask that. As shy a person as he is, he said yes right away."

"Reece, this is the greatest news. I could kiss your ass in Macy's window for getting this done."

We both laughed, and he added,

"That would be a sight, wouldn't it?"

"Reece, I'll keep in touch, and I wish Candy the best."

"That's an added bonus for me, John; we're getting along much better now."

As we were talking, I barely remembered walking out of the SAC with Genna and Reece. His car was parked the other way, so we said good-bye.

I was glad to hear Charlie's subconscious had been breached. I was continuing to have help along the way.

* * *

The colder weather was another reminder things were changing. We'd had summer-like temps almost until the exhibition game, but that abruptly changed like opening a freezer door in a hot garage. The cold is a sign of freshness, and exciting times for college sports fans; especially when the football and basketball seasons overlap. I enjoy watching both sports, but I'm in the minority that heavily favors the hoop over the pigskin.

The games before the Coastal East league play, the out of conference schedule, was a breeze for this year's team. Actually, it was more like a hurricane for the havoc they caused their opponents. The reason for this was because the two practice teams, team A, the starters, and team B, the reserve substitutes, were all Coastal East quality players. So practice was like a conference game. These teams they were running over were not Coastal East quality. Bloggers and beat writers were taking notice, and backtracking their earlier predictions of youthful growing pains, and as many wins as losses. Some of those BC members, who weren't willing to be as brazen as I, joined my bandwagon after I berated them for being late for the party. We were getting very near to the Ark shindig that would be uproarious enough to loosen some more paint flakes from that old ceiling. There would be more headaches than not after the event; anticipating the extracurricular event I would probably witness could lead to a mean hangover for me.

I needed to get to the Ark beforehand; there was something I had to find out. With another half fib to Genna, about taking care of something at the Ark before the rally, I headed up Route 20 once again. It was Thursday afternoon before the Saturday night event, and I needed to know the tenor of my ghostly friends, especially one in particular.

Upon my arrival through the back door, I noticed the folding chairs had not been put out yet. Also, easier in the headache department, there was no Mega vs. Sunny being played, again. Since no players were on the floor, I decided to check the supply room for any lost souls.

No luck there; I went past the locker room, and not hearing any showers, I headed for the player's lounge. There they all were, without a real person in sight, except me. They were each paired around the three pool tables, ever competing. I noticed the ball and cues were as invisible as they were. I whispered anyway,

"How come you guys aren't ballin?"

They all gave me a smile, while Slick plopped his cue down, and approached me.

"John, we don't feel like we're in limbo anymore. We almost feel alive again. There's no drudgery or chore like pain anymore. We all started to feel this way after you last talked to CB at the pool. Look at him. He's his old self, in spirit, and spirit!"

This last remark cracked us all up, while CB came over and tried to hug me; but we were like two puffs of smoke to each other. This caused another laugh.

"If you guys don't mind, can you spare Charlie? I'd like to talk to him alone."

"We can spare him now, but not for a game." Quincy chimed in with his usual humor. More laughs.

Charlie and I headed back to the supply room, the weigh station for so much of this saga. I still couldn't get over the demeanor of the six of them. There really was a transformation taking place. He sat at the edge of the table, and fixed his basset hound eyes on mine.

"How were you able to reach your today self?" realizing how odd that sounded.

"John, I'll try to explain it. I somehow was able to reach him in his dream. It was like we could see each other, we were both ghosts. Right after you saved me at the pool; I kept trying and trying to reach him that way. It took a long time before I succeeded. I didn't hear anyone say or instruct me to do this. My whole existence revolves around this old Ark, for about forty years. That was the first time I remember being out of here. I just felt I was being moved, like a chess piece, and there I was, in his dream."

I just smiled at all of this; a happy absurdity is the best way I can describe it.

"Charlie, when I said I would help you guys, it was a sincere hope, and I never gave up. I'm telling you, and you tell the other guys, play the game again this Saturday night."

I then looked into his hound dog eyes and said,

"Charlie, I didn't save you, I paid you back for saving me."

I went out the door, and was quickly on my way home again.

* * *

The event at the Ark had gone viral around the Campus. The Ark could have sold out many times over. Phineas "Ken" Barnum had the savvy idea of selling half price tickets to watch the event at the SAC on closed circuit TV, and THAT was almost sold out. Luckily, there were no other events scheduled that night at the SAC, or the BC would have lost a bundle.

It's very hard to describe the event. The elements of a Circus Maximus, combined with a school colored kaleidoscope is a beginning. Ken put quite a team together to organize the event. He blended the coaching staff, the current players, and past NCAA "dancing" players with the sideshow promotions that raised money for the basketball program, as well as the club. All the players that went to the Dance got their due, including my favorite ghosts. The pace was like a soft drum roll getting louder, leading to the base drums, and then crashing cymbals, as a wave that hits the shore.

On the crest of the wave was Charlie Bennett who was introduced by Larry Dariani, the AD who knew a bit more about Charlie's part in Sunny basketball history than Manny Wheaton, who stood politely next to Larry. CB waited his queue until Larry masterfully touched on Charlie's legend, so that everyone listening, young and old, felt they knew him. When the din died down, which could have been heard at the SAC without a sound system, CB, who was always a man of few words, said these:

"Thank you, I'm back, and I want to go dancing with all of you this year!"

The Ark shuddered like an earthquake.

All the while this was proceeding; I was privy to Sunnyside thrashing Megamont by thirty two points. Those Sunny ghosts played like gods.

Exhausted, the revelers gradually filtered out the doors of the Ark. Charlie Bennett was still being mobbed by fans and players alike. He started moving past me towards one of the exits. We made brief eye contact, but I didn't ring any bells in his head. I hadn't seen him in a couple of years, and then I was just a fan. I had no contact with him throughout this process with the Back Court.

You know what? I didn't care he didn't know or acknowledge my efforts on his behalf. If I had ten million dollars to build a new basketball court, I wouldn't want my name on the gift. "Anonymous" is better than "look at me."

The ghosts were leaving the court. While the Sunny players galloped toward the locker room, the Megamont team limped off the court like broken down mules. I sauntered toward the supply room, as if looking for a men's room. Once in, there were no players, or ghosts, I should say. However, I heard a lot of noise coming from the pool area.

Worth checking out, I thought.

The noise got louder as I approached the pool door. Once more, I just missed stepping in disinfectant.

It was quite a sight seeing six player ghosts swimming in the pool in celebration. I suddenly realized they weren't celebrating a win on the court, as they waved to me, and gradually dissolved into the water.

I stood silently until the pool water stopped lapping the sides, and calmed to a glassy, reflective stillness. I heard a faint noise of a shower in the distance, which became louder and louder….

Faint words were also getting louder, sounding like a traffic report. My eyes began to focus on our radio alarm clock on my bedside table. The time was 10:30 AM.

Epilogue

I lay on the bed, rolling my eyes, limply exhausted from what I couldn't remember. The shower I heard was Genna's, a rare out of bed before me occurrence. I scanned the room, and tried to think of the last thing I remembered.

The Back Court ... Calvin … Blogging … a "novel" idea … exhaustion. That was all I could think of.

I heard the shower stop. I could hear her toweling off, and grunting slightly at some of the aches and pains of our age. She appeared at the bedside in her robe.

"Well, you're up. What the hell were you dreaming about last night? You were thrashing around like you were in a street fight. At one point, you seemed to be having an epileptic fit. I tried to wake you, but I couldn't. All of a sudden, you calmed down, and became very serene. You even had a little smile on your face. Your breathing seemed normal, so I left you alone. I went to go sleep in the guest bedroom at around 3:00 A.M."

"Was I talking?"

"You were mumbling. All I could hear was 'Slick' before I got up and left. Does that ring a bell?"

"That's the nickname for Reece Sampson whom you and I have met at basketball banquets. He has the daughter that's a very good player. Why the hell was I dreaming about him?"

"Your dream. Don't ask me."

I slowly sat up in bed, because I felt like I was in a fight. I ached all over. Although it wasn't Sunday, this was going to be a day of rest for me. The walk would have to wait for tomorrow, as well as anything else that didn't have to get done today.

As Genna asked, what the hell was I dreaming? The one clue about Reece Sampson wasn't much help.

Ahh… just a minute. I can't remember referring to Slick Sampson by his given name, Reece, before this dream awakening. Still not much help.

I dragged myself into the bathroom and did what I had to do to wake up some more. I wasn't very hungry, so I sat down in my favorite sunny chair in the family room to offer some prayers. I say prayers for family, friends, and the good people of the world that need assistance. If you're in that group, you're in my prayers.

I need quiet to concentrate. I had this, as Genna was still in her bathroom creating beauty. However, I was still distracted by names entering my thoughts. Charlie … Harry … John … Quincy … These guys played with Slick about forty years ago, the best team Sunny ever had. They even played at the old Ark, before the SAC was even built. I knew the place well, because I cheered for a team five years before they played there.

It dawned on me that it was exactly forty years, and no ten year salute to them as was the custom. I made a mental note to my buddy Ken Blarney, the Back Court President, to see if something could still be done about that.

I managed to minimize distractions, and got through the rest of my wishes for good people. I moved into the kitchen into an equally sunny chair at the breakfast table. I skimmed the newspaper, past the nonsense to the entertainment section; the start of a little R&R I needed today. I noticed an advertisement for the play *Godspell,* which after about forty years of roaming the desert at out of the way venues, was returning to Broadway in New York City.

Gee, I thought, that's about how long the Sunny basketball program has had a meaningful presence in the NCAA tourney, or the "Dance." Another mental note to Ken; maybe the BC can have a promotion, in the old Ark honoring those former players, and making a few bucks to boot. After a bowl of cut fruit, banana, and cup of green tea (Tazo Zen), I gingerly headed to the small TV in the guest room. I plopped down on the bed that Genna used the night before, fleeing whatever battle I was engaged in. I began channel surfing in the digital age, remembering how convenient it is to not have to get up to change the dial, like back in the 70's. I was almost through the channel lineup when I came upon a *Twilight Zone* marathon, which I used to love as a kid.

The Occurrence at Owl Creek Bridge, a short story by Ambrose Bierce, was just beginning. What luck, I thought. This episode was among my top five of all Rod Serling's efforts, the creator of the TZ. It's the story of a Confederate soldier who is about to be hanged on Owl Creek Bridge, and what he imagines before the rope snaps, including his escape.

I began wondering if this was the kind of dream I had last night. I checked my stiff neck for rope burns. After the episode was over, I turned the TV off, and just sat up on the bed, motionless. After fifteen minutes, I forgot about the R&R, dressed as fast as Superman, kissed Genna, and headed for the car in the garage.

"Where are you going?"

"Be back soon. Don't worry."

I was driving reasonably fast north on Route 20; reasonably meaning a cop wouldn't notice me being reckless. Despite the aches and pains, I felt acutely aware; the twilight was gone.

I had to get to the Ark, but I really didn't know why. En route I had the feeling I'd been this way many times recently, and I hadn't. I remembered the Ark was a special place, a refuge for campus life with concerts and comedy acts to ease the stress of higher learning. It was also a crazy place, an asylum where crazy things happened....

I pulled into the lot behind, and I thought the car and I were on autopilot. I got out, and walked toward a specific back door; one of several, but I was drawn to this one. Inside, there was hardly a soul. I continued down the court sideline like I had a wind at my back, and stopped outside a door that said "Supply Room."

I entered, and saw a room that was ship shape; everything was in its place. I walked over to the desk in the corner, and noticed a single piece of copy paper that was magic markered with the word "Thanks."

I almost said, "You're welcome," because it felt like I did something good there. It was probably just a kind note to the cleaning person, in advance of them getting there.

"Excuse me. What are you doing here?"

This huge security guard was hunched over me as he waited for my answer. I fumbled,

"I was just reminiscing. I went to Sunny years ago ..."

"Well, you're going to have to reminisce outside. Only authorized personnel are allowed in here. I'll show you to the door, and make sure it's locked this time. Come with me."

I mumbled a "Sorry," as I passed through the doorway.

He said nothing, and I heard the lock click behind me.

I was still on autopilot on the way home; I hardly remember being on the road until I pulled into my garage.

"Where did you go? Are you alright?"

"I'm feeling fine now. I just had to get out for a drive. What are we doing?"

"Not much today, but tomorrow is the Fourth of July barbecue at the clubhouse. It should be fun."

"I agree. I'm looking forward to it."

I'm looking forward to a lot of writing. I hope it all comes back to me soon.

End

Made in the USA
Charleston, SC
28 August 2012